The Call of the Wild
The Cruise of the 'Dazzler'

The Call of the Wild
9

The Cruise of the 'Dazzler'
105

Jack London

octopus

Jack London was born illegitimate and in poverty in California in 1876. At fifteen he was the notorious 'Prince of the Oyster Pirates' on San Francisco Bay. At seventeen he shipped as a seaman on the *Sophie Sutherland* for Japan; later he served a term for vagrancy before joining the Klondike Gold Rush. He read voraciously and by the age of twenty-four was publishing in magazines; by thirty he was famous. In his relatively short writing career (1899–1916) he wrote over fifty books; he was also an ardent socialist, a pioneer in modern agriculture, a war correspondent in Korea and designed and sailed his own ship halfway round the world.

London's most famous work is contained in his stories of the far North based on his own experiences; he wrote other stories for children (*Tales of the Fish Patrol*, *The Cruise of the 'Dazzler'*) and he also wrote adult fiction, plays, travel sketches and important sociological books, the best known of which are *The People of the Abyss* and *John Barleycorn*.

He died in 1916, the world's first millionaire novelist.

This edition published in Great Britain in 1980 by
Octopus Books Limited
59 Grosvenor Street, London W1X 9DA

ISBN 0 7064 1323 7

© 1978 Illustrations Octopus Books Limited

Illustrated by Dan Pearce

Reprinted 1982

The Call of the Wild first published in 1903
The Cruise of the 'Dazzler' first published in 1902

The Call of the Wild

The Call of the Wild

Jack London

Contents

List of Illustrations

1 Into the Primitive

Old longings nomadic leap,
Chafing at custom's chain;
Again from its brumal sleep
Wakens the ferine strain.

Buck did not read the newspapers, or he would have known that trouble was brewing not alone for himself, but for every tide-water dog, strong of muscle and with warm, long hair, from Puget Sound to San Diego. Because men, groping in the Arctic darkness, had found a yellow metal, and because steamship and transportation companies were booming the find, thousands of men were rushing into the Northland. These men wanted dogs, and the dogs they wanted were heavy dogs, with strong muscles by which to toil and furry coats to protect them from the frost.

Buck lived at a big house in the sun-kissed Santa Clara Valley. Judge Miller's place, it was called. It stood back from the road, half hidden among the trees, through which glimpses could be caught of the wide cool veranda that ran around its four sides. The house was approached by gravelled driveways which wound about through wide-spreading lawns and under the interlacing boughs of tall poplars. At the rear things were on even a more spacious scale than at the front. There were great stables, where a dozen grooms and boys held forth, rows of vine-clad servants' cottages, an endless and orderly array of out-houses, long grape arbours, green pastures, orchards, and berry patches. Then there was the pumping plant for the artesian well, and the big cement tank where Judge Miller's boys took their morning plunge and kept cool in the hot afternoon.

And over this great demesne Buck ruled. Here he was born, and here he had lived the four years of his life. It was true, there were other dogs. There could not but be other dogs on so vast a place, but they did not count. They came and went, resided in the populous kennels, or lived obscurely in the recesses of the house after the fashion of Toots, the Japanese pug, or Ysabel, the Mexican hairless – strange creatures that rarely put nose out of doors or set foot to ground. On the other hand, there were the fox terriers, a score of them at least, who yelped fearful promises at Toots and Ysabel looking out of the windows at them and protected by a legion of housemaids armed with brooms and mops.

But Buck was neither house-dog nor kennel-dog. The whole realm was his. He plunged into the swimming tank or went hunting with the Judge's sons; he escorted Mollie and Alice, the Judge's daughters, on long twilight or early morning rambles; on wintry nights he lay at the Judge's feet before the roaring library fire; he carried the Judge's grandsons on his back, or rolled them in the grass, and guarded their footsteps through wild adventures down to the fountain in the stable yard, and even beyond, where the paddocks were, and the berry patches. Among the terriers he stalked imperiously, and Toots and Ysabel he utterly ignored, for he was king – king over all the creeping, crawling, flying things of Judge Miller's place, humans included.

His father, Elmo, a huge St Bernard, had been the Judge's inseparable companion and Buck did fair to follow in the way of his father. He was not so large – he weighed only one hundred and forty pounds – for his mother, Shep, had been a Scotch shepherd dog. Nevertheless, one hundred and forty pounds, to which was added the dignity that comes of good living and universal respect, enabled him to carry himself in right royal fashion. During the four years since his puppyhood he had lived the life of a sated aristocrat; he had a fine pride in himself, was ever a trifle egotistical, as country gentlemen sometimes become because of their insular situation. But he had saved himself by not becoming a mere pampered house-dog. Hunting and kindred outdoor delights had kept down the fat and hardened his muscles; and to him, as to the cold-tubbing races, the love of water had been a tonic and a health preserver.

And this was the manner of dog Buck in the fall of 1897, when the Klondike strike dragged men from all the world into the frozen North. But Buck did not read the newspapers, and he did not know that Manuel, one of the gardener's helpers, was an undesirable acquaintance. Manuel had one besetting sin. He loved to play Chinese lottery. Also, in his gambing, he had one besetting weakness – faith in a system; and this made his damnation certain. For to play a system requires money, while the wages of a gardener's helper do not lap over the needs of a wife and numerous progeny.

The Judge was at a meeting of the Raisin Growers' Association, and the boys were busy organising an athletic club, on the memorable night of Manuel's treachery. No one saw him and Buck go off through the orchard on what Buck imagined was merely a stroll. And with the exception of a solitary man, no one saw them arrive at the little flag station known as College Park. This man talked with Manuel, and money clinked between them.

'You might wrap up the goods before you deliver 'm,' the stranger said gruffly, and Manuel doubled a piece of stout rope around Buck's neck under the collar.

'Twist it, an' you'll choke 'm plentee,' said Manuel, and the stranger grunted a ready affirmative.

Buck had accepted the rope with quiet dignity. To be sure, it was an unwonted performance: but he had learned to trust in men he knew, and to give them credit for a wisdom that outreached his own. But when the ends of the rope were placed in the stranger's hands, he growled menacingly. He had merely intimated his displeasure, in his pride believing that to intimate was to command. But to his surprise the rope tightened around his neck, shutting off his breath. In quick rage he sprang at the man, who met him halfway, grappled him close by the throat, and with a deft twist threw him over on his back. Then the rope tightened mercilessly, while Buck struggled in a fury, his tongue lolling out of his mouth and his great chest panting futilely. Never in all his life had he been so vilely treated, and never in all his life had he been so angry. But his strength ebbed, his eyes glazed, and he knew nothing when the train was flagged and the two men threw him into the baggage car.

The next he knew, he was dimly aware that his tongue was hurting and that he was being jolted along in some kind of conveyance. The hoarse shriek of a locomotive whistling a crossing told him where he was. He had travelled too often with the Judge not to know the sensation of riding in a baggage car. He opened his eyes, and into them came the unbridled anger of a kidnapped king. The man sprang for his throat, but Buck was too quick for him. His jaws closed on the hand; nor did they relax till his senses were choked out of him once more.

'Yep, has fits,' the man said, hiding his mangled hand from the baggageman, who had been attracted by the sounds of struggle. 'I'm takin' 'im up for the boss to 'Frisco. A crack dog-doctor there thinks that he can cure 'im.'

Concerning that night's ride the man spoke most eloquently for himself, in a little shed back of a saloon on the San Francisco water front.

'All I get is fifty for it,' he grumbled; 'an' I wouldn't do it over for a thousand, cold cash.'

His hand was wrapped in a bloody handkerchief, and the right trouser leg was ripped from knee to ankle.

'How much did the other mug get?' the saloon-keeper demanded.

'A hundred,' was the reply. 'Wouldn't take a sou less, so help me.'

'That makes a hundred and fifty,' the saloon-keeper calculated, 'and he's worth it, or I'm a squarehead.'

The kidnapper undid the bloody wrappings and looked at his lacerated hand. 'If I don't get the hydrophoby——'

'It'll be because you were born to hang,' laughed the saloon-keeper. 'Here, lend me a hand before you pull your freight,' he added.

Dazed, suffering intolerable pain from throat and tongue, with the life half throttled out of him, Buck attempted to face his tormentors. But he was thrown down and choked repeatedly, till they succeeded in filing the heavy brass collar from off his neck. Then the rope was removed, and he was flung into a cage-like crate.

There he lay for the remainder of the weary night, nursing his wrath and wounded pride. He could not understand what it all meant. What did they want with him, these strange men? Why were they keeping him pent up in this narrow crate? He did not know why, but he felt oppressed by the vague sense of impending calamity. Several times during the night he sprang to his feet when the shed door rattled open, expecting to see the Judge, or the boys at least. But each time it was the bulging face of the saloon-keeper that peered in at him by the sickly light of a tallow candle. And each time the joyful bark that trembled in Buck's throat was twisted into a savage growl.

But the saloon-keeper let him alone, and in the morning four men entered and picked up the crate. More tormentors, Buck decided, for they were evil-looking creatures, ragged and unkempt; and he stormed and raged at them through the bars. They only laughed and poked sticks at him, which he promptly assailed with his teeth till he realised that that was what they wanted. Whereupon he lay down sullenly and allowed the crate to be lifted into a waggon. Then he, and the crate in which he was imprisoned, began a passage through many hands. Clerks in the express office took charge of him; he was carted about in another waggon; a truck carried him, with an assortment of boxes and parcels, upon a ferry steamer; he was trucked off the steamer into a great railway depot, and finally he was deposited in an express car.

For two days and nights this express car was dragged along at the tail of shrieking locomotives; and for two days and nights Buck neither ate nor drank. In his anger he had met the first advances of the express messengers with growls, and they had retaliated by teasing him. When he flung himself against the bars, quivering and frothing, they laughed at him and taunted him. They growled and barked like detestable dogs, mewed, and flapped their arms and crowed. It was all very silly, he knew; but therefore the more outrage to his dignity, and his anger waxed and waxed. He did not mind the hunger so much, but the lack of water caused him severe suffering and fanned his wrath to fever-pitch. For that matter, high-strung and finely sensitive, the ill treatment had flung him into a fever, which was fed by the imflammation of his parched and swollen throat and tongue.

He was glad for one thing: the rope was off his neck. That had given them an unfair advantage; but now that it was off, he would show them. They would never get another rope around his neck. Upon that he was resolved. For two days and nights he neither ate nor drank, and during those two days and nights of torment, he accumulated a fund of wrath that boded ill for whoever first fell foul of him. His eyes turned bloodshot, and he was metamorphosed into a raging fiend. So changed was he that the Judge himself would not have recognised him; and the express messengers breathed with relief when they bundled him off the train at Seattle.

Four men gingerly carried the crate from the waggon into a small, high-walled backyard. A stout man, with a red sweater that sagged generously at the neck, came out and signed the book for the driver. That was the man, Buck divined, the next tormentor, and he hurled himself savagely against the bars. The man smiled grimly, and brought a hatchet and a club.

'You ain't goning to take him out now?' the driver asked.

'Sure,' the man replied, driving the hatchet into the crate for a pry.

There was an instantaneous scattering of the four men who had carried it in, and from safe perches on top the wall they prepared to watch the performance.

Buck rushed at the splintering wood, sinking his teeth into it, surging and wrestling with it. Wherever the hatchet fell on the outside, he was there on the inside, snarling and growling, as furiously anxious to get out as the man in the red sweater was calmly intent on getting him out.

'Now, you red-eyed devil,' he said, when he had made an opening sufficient for the passage of Buck's body. At the same time he dropped the hatchet and shifted the club to his right hand.

And Buck was truly a red-eyed devil, as he drew himself together for the spring, hair bristling, mouth foaming, a mad glitter in his blood-shot eyes. Straight at the man he launched his one hundred and forty pounds of fury, surcharged with the pent passion of two days and

Buck rushed at the splintering wood, sinking his teeth into it

nights. In mid air, just as his jaws were about to close on the man, he received a shock that checked his body and brought his teeth together with an agonising clip. He whirled over, fetching the ground on his back and side. He had never been struck by a club in his life, and did not understand. With a snarl that was part bark and more scream he was again on his feet and launched into the air. And again the shock came and he was brought crushingly to the ground. This time he was aware that it was the club, but his madness knew no caution. A dozen times he charged, and as often the club broke the charge and smashed him down.

After a particularly fierce blow, he crawled to his feet, too dazed to rush. He staggered limply about, the blood flowing from nose and mouth and ears, his beautiful coat sprayed and flecked with bloody slaver. Then the man advanced and deliberately dealt him a frightful blow on the nose. All the pain he had endured was as nothing compared with the exquisite agony of this. With a roar that was almost lionlike in it ferocity, he again hurled himself at the man. But the man, shifting the club from right to left, coolly caught him by the the under jaw, at the same time wrenching downward and backward. Buck described a complete circle in the air, and half of another, then crashed to the ground on his head and chest.

For the last time he rushed. The man struck the shrewd blow he had purposely withheld for so long, and Buck crumpled up and went down, knocked utterly senseless.

'He's no slouch at dog-breakin', that's wot I say,' one of the men on the wall cried enthusiastically.

'Druther break cayuses any day, and twice on Sundays,' was the reply of the driver, as he climbed on the waggon and started the horses.

Buck's senses came back to him, but not his strength. He lay where he had fallen, and from there he watched the man in the red sweater.

'"Answers to to the name of Buck,"' the man soliloquised, quoting from the saloon-keeper's letter which had announced the consignment of the crate and contents. 'Well, Buck, my boy,' he went on in a genial voice, 'we've had our little ruction, and the best thing we can do is to let it go at that. You've learned your place, and I know mine. Be a bad dog, and all 'll go well and the goose hang high. Be a bad dog, and I'll whale the stuffin' outa you. Understand?'

As he spoke he fearlessly patted the head he had so mercilessly pounded, and though Buck's hair involuntarily bristled at touch of the hand, he endured it without protest. When the man brought water he drank eagerly, and later bolted a generous meal of raw meat, chunk by chunk, from the man's hand.

He was beaten (he knew that); but he was not broken. He saw, once for all, that he stood no chance against a man with a club. He had learned the lesson, and in all his after life he never forgot it. That club was a revelation. It was his introduction to the reign of primitive law, and he met the introduction halfway. The facts of life took on a fiercer aspect; and while he faced that aspect uncowed, he faced it with all the latent cunning of his nature aroused. As the days went by, other dogs came in crates and at the ends of ropes, some docilely, and some raging and roaring as he had come; and, one and all, he watched them pass under the dominion of the man in the red sweater. Again and again, as he looked at each brutal performance, the lesson was driven home to Buck: a man with a club was a lawgiver, a master to be obeyed, though not necessarily conciliated. Of this last Buck was never guilty, though he did see beaten dogs that fawned upon the man, and wagged their tails, and licked his hand. Also he saw one dog, that would neither conciliate nor obey, finally killed in the struggle for mastery.

Now and again men came, strangers, who talked excitedly, wheedlingly, and in all kinds of fashions to the man in the red sweater. And at such times that money passed between them the stranger took one or more of the dogs away with them. Buck wondered where they went, for they never came back; but the fear of the future was strong upon him, and he was glad each time when he was not selected.

Yet his time came, in the end, in the form of a little weazened man who spat broken English and many strange and uncouth exclamations which Buck could not understand.

'Sacredam!' he cried, when his eyes lit upon Buck. 'Dat one dam bully dog! Eh? How moch?'

'Three hundred, and a present at that,' was the prompt reply of the man in the red sweater. 'And seein' it's government money, you ain't got no kick coming; eh, Perrault?'

Perrault grinned. Considering that the price of dogs had been boomed skyward by the unwonted demand, it was not an unfair sum for so fine an animal. The Canadian Government would be no loser, nor would its despatches travel the slower. Perrault knew dogs, and when he looked at Buck he knew that he was one in a thousand – 'One in ten t'ousand,' he commented mentally.

Buck saw money pass between them, and was not surprised when Curly, a good-natured Newfoundland, and he were led away by the little weazened man. That was the last he saw of the man in the red sweater, and as Curly and he looked at receding Seattle from the deck of the *Narwhal*, it was the last he saw of the warm Southland. Curly and he were taken below by Perrault and turned over to a black-faced giant called Francois. Perrault was a French-Canadian, and swarthy; but Francois was a French-Canadian half-breed, and twice as swarthy. They were a new kind of men to Buck (of which he was destined to see many more), and while he developed no affection for them, he none the less grew honestly to respect them. He speedily learned that Perrault and François were fair men, calm and impartial in administering justice, and too wise in the way of dogs to be ever fooled by dogs.

In the 'tween-decks of the *Narwhal*, Buck and Curly joined two other dogs. One of them was a big, snow-white fellow from Spitzbergen who had been brought away by a whaling captain, and who had later accompanied a Geological Survey into the Barrens. He was friendly, in a treacherous sort of way, smiling into one's face the while he meditated some underhand trick, as, for instance, when he stole from Buck's food at the first meal. As Buck sprang to punish him, the lash of François whip sang through the air, reaching the culprit first; and nothing remained to Buck but to recover the bone. That was fair of Francois, he decided, and the half-breed began to rise in Buck's estimation.

The other dog made no advance, nor received any; also, he did not attempt to steal from the newcomers. He was a gloomy, morose fellow, and he showed Curly plainly that all he desired was to be left alone, and further, that there would be trouble if he were not left alone. 'Dave' he was called, and he ate and slept, or yawned between times, and took interest in nothing, not even when the *Narwhal* crossed Queen Charlotte Sound and rolled and pitched and bucked like a thing possessed. When Buck and Curly grew excited, half wild with fear, he raised his head as though annoyed, favoured them with an incurious glance, yawned, and went to sleep again.

Day and night the ship throbbed to the tireless pulse of the propeller, and though one day was very like another, it was apparent to Buck that the weather was steadily growing colder. At last, one morning, the propeller was quiet, and the *Narwhal* was pervaded with an atmosphere of excitement. He felt it, as did the other dogs, and knew that a change was at hand. François leashed them and brought them on deck. At the first step upon the cold surface, Buck's feet sank into a white mushy something very like mud. He sprang back with a snort. More of this white stuff was falling through the air. He shook himself, but more of it fell upon him. He sniffed it curiously, then licked some up on his tongue. It bit like fire, and the next instant was gone. This puzzled him. He tried it again, with the same result. The onlookers laughed uproariously, and he felt ashamed, he knew not why, for it was his first snow.

2   The Law of Club and Fang

Buck's first day on the Dyea beach was like a nightmare. Every hour was filled with shock and surprise. He had been suddenly jerked from the heart of civilisation and flung into the heart of things primordial. No lazy, sun-kissed life was this, with nothing to do but loaf and be bored. Here was neither peace, nor rest, nor a moment's safety. All was confusion and action, and every moment life and limb were in peril. There was imperative need to be constantly alert; for these dogs and men were not town dogs and men. They were savages, all of them; who knew no law but the law of club and fang.

He had never seen dogs fight as these wolfish creatures fought, and his first experience taught him an unforgetable lesson. It is true, it was a vicarious experience, else he would not have lived to profit by it. Curly was the victim. They were camped near the log store, where she, in her friendly way, made advances to a husky dog the size of a full-grown wolf, though not half so large as she. There was no warning, only a leap in like a flash, a metallic clip of teeth, a leap out equally swift, and Curly's face was ripped open from eye to jaw.

It was the wolf manner of fighting, to strike and leap away; but there was more to it than this. Thirty or forty huskies ran to the spot and surrounded the combatants in an intent and silent circle. Buck did not comprehend that silent intentness, nor the eager way with which they were licking their chops. Curly rushed her antagonist, who struck again and leaped aside. He met her next rush with his chest, in a peculiar fashion that tumbled her off her feet. She never regained them. This was what the onlooking huskies had waited for. They closed in upon her, snarling and yelping, and she was buried, screaming with agony, beneath the bristling mass of bodies.

So sudden was it, and so unexpected, that Buck was taken aback. He saw Spitz run out his scarlet tongue in a way he had of laughing; and he saw François, swinging an axe, spring into the mess of dogs. Three men with clubs were helping him to scatter them. It did not take long. Two minutes from the time Curly went down, the last of her assailants were clubbed off. But she lay there limp and lifeless in the bloody, trampled snow, almost literally torn to pieces, the swart half-breed standing over her and cursing horribly. The scene often came back to Buck to trouble him in his sleep. So that was the way. No fair play. Once down, that was the end of you. Well, he would see to it that he never went down. Spitz ran out his tongue and laughed again and from that moment Buck hated him with a bitter and deathless hatred.

Before he had recovered from the shock caused by the tragic passing of Curly, he received another shock. François fastened upon him an arrangement of straps and buckles. It was a harness, such as he had seen the grooms put on the horses at home. And as he had seen horses work, so he was set to work, hauling Francois on a sled to the forest that fringed the valley, and returning with a load of firewood. Though his dignity was sorely hurt by thus being made a draught animal, he was too wise to rebel. He buckled down with a will and did his best, though it was all new and strange. François was stern, demanding instant obedience; and by virtue of his whip receiving instant obedience; while Dave, who was an experienced wheeler, nipped Buck's hind quarters whenever he was in error. Spitz was the leader, likewise experienced, and while he could not always get at Buck, he growled sharp reproof now and again, or cunningly threw his weight in the traces to jerk Buck into the way he should go. Buck learned easily, and under the combined tuition of his two mates and François made remarkable progress. Ere they returned to camp he knew enough to stop at 'ho,' to go ahead at 'mush,' to swing wide on the bends; and to keep clear of the wheeler when the loaded sled shot downhill at their heels.

'T'ree vair' good dogs,' François told Perrault. 'Dat Buck, heem pool lak hell, I tich heem queek as anyt'ing.'

By afternoon, Perrault, who was in a hurry to be on the trail with his despatches, returned with two more dogs. 'Billee' and 'Joe' he called them, two brothers, and true huskies both. Sons of the one mother though they were, they were as different as day and night. Billee's one fault was his excessive good nature, while Joe was the very opposite, sour and introspective, with a perpetual snarl and a malignant eye. Buck received them in comradely fashion. Dave ignored them; while Spitz proceeded to thrash first one and then the other. Billee wagged his tail appeasingly, turned to run when he saw that appeasement was of no avail, and cried (still appeasingly) when Spitz's sharp teeth scored his flank. But no matter how Spitz circled, Joe whirled around on his heels to face him, mane bristling, ears laid back, lips writhing and snarling, jaws clipping together as fast as he could snap, and eyes diabolically gleaming – the incarnation of belligerent fear. So terrible was his appearance that Spitz was forced to forego disciplining him; but to cover his own discomfiture he turned upon the inoffensive and wailing Billee and drove him to the confines of the camp.

By evening Perrault secured another dog, an old husky, long and lean and gaunt, with a battle-scarred face and a single eye which flashed a warning of prowess that commanded respect. He was called Sol-leks, which means the Angry One. Like Dave, he asked nothing, gave nothing, expected nothing; and when he marched slowly and deliberately into their midst, even Spitz left him alone. He had one peculiarity which Buck was unlucky enough to discover. He did not like to be approached on his blind side. Of this offence Buck was unwittingly guilty, and the first knowledge he had of his indiscretion was when Sol-leks whirled upon him and slashed his shoulder to the bone for three inches up and down. Forever after Buck avoided his blind side, and to the last of their comradeship had no more trouble. His only apparent ambition, like Dave's, was to be left alone; though, as Buck was afterward to learn, each of them possessed one other and even more vital ambition.

That night Buck faced the great problem of sleeping. The tent,

illumined by a candle, glowed warmly in the midst of the white plain;
and when he, as a matter of course, entered it, both Perrault and François bombarded him with curses and cooking utensils till he recovered
from his consternation and fled ignominiously into the outer cold. A
chill wind was blowing that nipped him sharply and bit with especial
venom into his wounded shoulder. He lay down on the snow and
attempted to sleep, but the frost soon drove him shivering to his feet.
Miserable and disconsolate, he wandered about among the many
tents, only to find that one place was as cold as another. Here and there
savage dogs rushed upon him, but he bristled his neck-hair and
snarled (for he was learning fast), and they let him go his way
unmolested.

Finally an idea came to him. He would return and see how his own
team-mates were making out. To his astonishment, they had disappeared. Again he wandered about through the great camp, looking for
them, again he returned. Were they in the tent? No, that could not be,
else he would not have been driven out. Then where could they
possibly be? With dropping tail and shivering body, very forlorn
indeed, he aimlessly circled the tent. Suddenly the snow gave way
beneath his fore legs and he sank down. Something wriggled under his
feet. He sprang back, bristling and snarling, fearful of the unseen and
unknown. But a friendly little yelp reassured him, and he went back to
investigate. A whiff of warm air ascended to his nostrils, and there,
curled up under the snow in a snug ball, lay Billee. He whined
placatingly, squirmed and wriggled to show his good will and
intention, and even ventured, as a bribe for peace, to lick Buck's face
with his warm wet tongue.

Another lesson. So that was the way they did it, eh? Buck
confidently selected a spot, and with much fuss and waste effort
proceeded to dig a hole for himself. In a trice the heat from his body
filled the confined space and he was asleep. The day had been long
and arduous, and he slept soundly and comfortably, though he
growled and barked and wrestled with bad dreams.

Nor did he open his eyes till roused by the noises of the waking
camp. At first he did not know where he was. It had snowed during the

night and he was completely buried. The snow walls pressed him on every side, and a great surge of fear swept through him – the fear of the wild thing for the trap. It was a token that he was harking back through his own life to the lives of his forebears; for he was a civilised dog, an unduly civilised dog, and of his own experience knew no trap and so could not of himself fear it. The muscles of his whole body contracted spasmodically and instinctively, the hair on his neck and shoulders stood on end, and with a ferocious snarl he bounded straight up into the blinding day, the snow flying about him in a flashing cloud. Ere he landed on his feet, he saw the white camp spread out before him and knew where he was and remembered all that had passed from the time he went for a stroll with Manuel to the hole he had dug for himself the night before.

A shout from François hailed his appearance. 'Wot I say?' the dog-driver cried to Perrault. 'Dat Buck for sure learn queek as anyt'ing.'

Perrault nodded gravely. As courier for the Canadian Government, bearing important despatches, he was anxious to secure the best dogs, and he was particularly gladdened by the possession of Buck.

Three more huskies were added to the team inside an hour, making a total of nine, and before another quarter of an hour had passed they were in harness and swinging up the trail toward the Dyea Cañon. Buck was glad to be gone, and though the work was hard he found he did not particularly despise it. He was surprised at the eagerness which animated the whole team and which was communicated to him; but still more surprising was the change wrought in Dave and Sol-leks. They were new dogs, utterly transformed by the harness. All passiveness and unconcern had dropped from them. They were alert and active, anxious that the work should go well and fiercely irritable with whatever, by delay or confusion, retarded that work. The toil of the traces seemed the supreme expression of their being, and all that they lived for and the only thing in which they took delight.

Dave was wheeler of sled dog, pulling in front of him was Buck, then came Sol-leks; the rest of the team was strung out ahead, single file, to the leader, which position was filled by Spitz.

Buck had been purposely placed between Dave and Sol-leks so that he might receive instruction. Apt scholar that he was, they were equally apt teachers, never allowing him to linger long in error, and enforcing their teaching with sharp teeth. Dave was fair and very wise. He never nipped Buck without cause, and he never failed to nip him when he stood in need of it. As Francois's whip backed him up, Buck found it to be cheaper to mend his ways than to retaliate. Once, during a brief halt, when he got tangled in the traces and delayed the start, both Dave and Sol-leks flew at him and administered a sound trouncing. The resulting tangle was even worse; but Buck took good care to keep the traces clear thereafter; and ere the day was done, so well had he mastered his work, his mates about ceased nagging him. François's whip snapped less frequently, and Perrault even honoured Buck by lifting up his feet and carefully examining them.

It was a hard day's run, up the Cañon, through Sheep Camp, past the Scales and timber line, across glaciers and snowdrifts hundreds of feet deep, and over the great Chilcoot Divide, which stands between the salt water and the fresh, and guards forbiddingly the sad and lonely North. They made good time down the chain of lakes which fills the craters of extinct volcanoes, and late that night pulled into the huge camp at the head of Lake Bennett, where thousands of gold-seekers were building boats against the break-up of the ice in the spring. Buck made his hole in the snow and slept the sleep of the exhausted just, but all too early was routed out in the cold darkness and harnessed with his mates to the sled.

That day they made forty miles, the trail being packed; but the next day, and for many days to follow, they broke their own trail, worked harder, and made poorer time. As a rule, Perrault travelled ahead of the team, packing the snow with webbed shoes to make it easier for them. Francois, guiding the sled at the geepole, sometimes exchanged places with him, but not often. Perrault was in a hurry, and he prided himself on his knowledge of ice, which knowledge was indispensable, for the fall ice was very thin, and where there was swift water, there was no ice at all.

Day after day, for days unending, buck toiled in the traces. Always they broke camp in the dark, and the first grey of dawn found them hitting the trail with fresh miles reeled off behind them. And always they pitched camp after dark, eating their bit of fish, and crawling to sleep into the snow. Buck was ravenous. The pound and a half of sundried salmon, which was his ration for each day, seemed to go nowhere. He never had enough, and suffered from perpetual hunger pangs. Yet the other dogs, because they weighed less and were born to the life, received a pound only of the fish and managed to keep in good condition.

He swiftly lost the fastidiousness which had characterised his old life. A dainty eater, he found that his mates, finishing first, robbed him of his unfinished ration. There was no defending it. While he was fighting off two or three, it was disappearing down the throats of the others. To remedy this, he ate as fast as they; and, so greatly did hunger compel him, he was not above taking what did not belong to him. He watched and learned. When he saw Pike, one of the new dogs, a clever malingerer and thief, slyly steal a slice of bacon when Perrault's back was turned, he duplicated the performance the following day, getting away with the whole chunk. A great uproar was raised, but he was unsuspected; while Dub, an awkward blunderer who was always getting caught, was punished for Buck's misdeed.

This first theft marked Buck as fit to survive in the hostile Northland environment. It marked his adaptability, his capacity to adjust himself to changing conditions, the lack of which would have meant swift and terrible death. It marked further the decay or going to pieces of his moral nature, a vain thing and a handicap in the ruthless struggle for existence. It was all well enough in the Southland, under the law of love and fellowship, to respect private property and personal feelings; but in the Northland, under the law of club and fang, whoso took such things into account was a fool, and in so far as he observed them he would fail to prosper.

Not that Buck reasoned it out. He was fit, that was all, and unconsciously he accommodated himself to the new mode of life. All his days, no matter what the odds, he had never run from a fight. But the club of the man in the red sweater had beaten into him a more fundamental and primitive code. Civilised, he could have died for a moral consideration, say the defence of Judge Miller's riding-whip; but the completeness of his decivilisation was not evidenced by his ability to flee from the defence of a moral consideration and so save his hide. He did not steal for joy of it, but because of the clamour of his stomach. He did not rob openly, but stole secretly and cunningly, out of respect for club and fang. In short, the things he did were done because it was easier to do them than not to do them.

His development (or retrogression) was rapid. His muscles became hard as iron, and he grew callous to all ordinary pain. He achieved an internal as well as external economy. He could eat anything, no matter how loathsome or indigestible; and, once eaten, the juices of his stomach extracted the last least particle of nutriment; and his blood carried it to the farthest reaches of his body, building it into the toughest and stoutest of tissues. Sight and scent became remarkably keen, while his hearing developed such acuteness that in his sleep he heard the faintest sound whether it heralded peace or peril. He learned to bite the ice out with his teeth when it collected between his toes; and when he was thirsty and there was a thick scum of ice over the water hole, he would break it by rearing and striking it with stiff fore legs. His most conspicious trait was an ability to scent the wind and forecast it a night in advance. No matter how breathless the air when he dug his nest by tree or bank, the wind that later blew inevitably found him to leeward, sheltered and snug.

And not only did he learn by experience, but instincts long dead became alive again. The domesticated generations fell from him. In vague ways he remembered back to the youth of the breed, to the time the wild dogs ranged in packs through the primeval forest and killed their meat as they ran it down. It was no task for him to learn to fight with cut and slash and the quick wolf snap. In this manner had fought forgotten ancestors. They quickened the old life within him, and the old tricks which they had stamped into the heredity of the breed were his tricks. They came to him without effort or discovery, as though they had been his always. And when, on the still cold nights, he pointed his nose at a star and howled long and wolflike, it was his ancestors, dead and dust, pointing nose at star and howling down through the centuries and through him. And his cadences were their cadences, the cadences which voiced their woe and what to them was the meaning of the stillness, and the cold, and dark.

Thus, as token of what a puppet thing life is, the ancient song surged through him and he came into his own again; and he came because men had found a yellow metal in the North, and because Manuel was a gardener's helper whose wages did not lap over the needs of his wife and divers small copies of himself which he had managed to accumulate.

3   The Dominant Primordial Beast

The dominant primordial beast was strong in Buck, and under the fierce conditions of trail life it grew and grew. Yet it was a secret growth. His new-born cunning gave him poise and control. He was too busy adjusting himself to the new life to feel at ease, and not only did he not pick fights, but he avoided them whenever possible. A certain deliberateness characterised his attitude. He was not prone to rashness and precipitate action; and in the bitter hatred between him and Spitz he betrayed no impatience, shunned all offensive acts.

On the other hand, possibly because he divined in Buck a dangerous rival, Spitz never lost an opportunity of showing his teeth. He even went out of his way to bully Buck, striving constantly to start the fight which could end only in the death of one or the other. Early in the trip this might have taken place had it not been for an unwonted accident. At the end of this day they made a bleak and miserable camp on the shore of Lake Le Barge. Driving snow, a wind that cut like a white-hot knife, and darkness had forced them to grope for a camping place. They could hardly have fared worse. At their backs rose a perpendicular wall of rock, and Perrault and François were compelled to make their fire and spread their sleeping robes on the ice of the lake itself. The tent they had discarded at Dyea in order to travel light. A few sticks of driftwood furnished them with a fire that thawed down through the ice and left them to eat supper in the dark.

Close in under the sheltering rock Buck made his nest. So snug and warm was it, that he was loath to leave it when Francois distributed the fish which he had first thawed over the fire. But when Buck finished his ration and returned, he found his nest occupied. A warning snarl told him that his trespasser was Spitz. Till now Buck had avoided trouble with his enemy, but this was too much. The beast in him roared. He sprang upon Spitz with a fury which surprised them both, and Spitz particularly, for his whole experience with Buck had gone to teach him that his rival was an unusually timid dog, who managed to hold his own because of his great weight and size.

François was surprised, too, when they shot out in a tangle from the disrupted nest and he divined the cause of the trouble. 'A-a-ah!' he cried to Buck. 'Gif it to heem , by Gar! Gif it to heem, the dirty t'eef!'

Spitz was equally willing. He was crying with sheer rage and eagerness as he circled back and forth for a chance to spring in. Buck was no less eager, and no less cautious, as he likewise circled back and forth for the advantage. But it was then the unexpected happened, the thing which projected their struggle for supremacy far into the future, past many a weary mile of trail and toil.

An oath from Perrault, the resounding impact of a club upon a bony frame, and a shrill yelp of pain, heralded the breaking forth of pandemonium. The camp was suddenly discovered to be alive with skulking furry forms – starving huskies, four or five score of them, who had scented the camp from some Indian village. They had crept in while Buck and Spitz were fighting, and when the two men sprang among them with stout clubs they showed their teeth and fought back. They were crazed by the smell of the food. Perrault found one with head buried in the grub-box. His club landed heavily on the gaunt ribs, and the grub-box was capsized on the ground. On the instant a score of the famished brutes were scrambling for the bread and bacon. The clubs fell upon them unheeded. They yelped and howled under the rain of blows, but struggled none the less madly till the last crumb had been devoured.

In the meantime the astonished team-dogs had burst out of their nests only to be set upon by the fierce invaders. Never had Buck seen such dogs. It seemed as though their bones would burst through their skins. They were mere skeletons, draped loosely in draggled hides, with blazing eyes and slavered fangs. But the hunger-madness made them terrifying, irresistible. There was no opposing them. The team-dogs were swept back against the cliff at the first onset. Buck was beset by three huskies, and in a trice his head and shoulders were ripped and slashed. The din was frightful. Billee was crying as usual. Dave and Sol-leks, dripping blood from a score of wounds, were fighting bravely side by side. Joe was snapping like a demon. Once, his teeth close on the fore leg of a husky, and he crunched down through the bone. Pike, the malingerer, leaped upon the crippled animal, breaking its neck with a quick flash of teeth and a jerk. Buck got a frothing adversary by the throat, and was sprayed with blood when his teeth sank through the jugular. The warm taste of it in his mouth goaded him to greater fierceness. He flung himself upon another, and at the same time felt teeth sink in his own throat. It was Spitz, treacherously attacking from the side.

Perrault and François, having cleaned out their part of the camp, hurried to save their sled-dogs. The wild wave of famished beasts rolled back before them, and Buck shook himself free. But it was only for a moment. The two men were compelled to run back to save the grub, upon which the huskies returned to the attack on the team. Billee, terrified into bravery, sprang through the savage circle and fled away over the ice. Pike and Cub followed on his heels, with the rest of the team behind. As Buck drew himself together to spring after them, out of the tail of his eye he saw Spitz rush upon him with the evident intention of overthrowing him. Once off his feet and under that mass of huskies, there was no hope for him. But he braced himself to the shock of Spitz's charge, then joined the flight out on the lake.

Later, the nine team-dogs gathered together and sought shelter in the forest. Though unpursued, they were in sorry plight. There was not one who was not wounded in four or five places, while some were wounded grievously. Dub was badly injured in a hind leg; Dolly, the last husky added to the team at Dyea, had a badly torn throat; Joe had lost an eye; while Billee, the good-natured, with an ear chewed and rent to ribbons, cried and whimpered throughout the night. At daybreak they limped warily back to camp, to find the marauders gone and the two men in bad tempers. Fully half their grub supply was gone. The huskies had chewed through the sled lashings and canvas covering. In fact, nothing, no matter how remotely eatable, had escaped them. They had eaten a pair of Perrault's moose-hide moccasins, chunks out of the leather traces, and even two feet of lash from the end of François's whip. He broke from a mournful contemplation of it to look over his wounded dogs.

'Ah, my frien's,' he said softly, 'mebbe it mek you mad dog, dose many bites. Mebbe all mad dog, sacredam! Wot you t'ink, eh, Perrault?'

The courier shook his head dubiously. With four hundred miles of trail still between him and Dawson, he could ill afford to have madness break out among his dogs. Two hours of cursing and exertion got the harness into shape, and the wound-stiffened team was under way, struggling painfully over the hardest part of the trail they had yet encountered, and for that matter, the hardest between them and Dawson.

The Thirty Mile River was wide open. Its wild water defied the frost, and it was in the eddies only and in the quiet places that the ice held at all. Six days of exhausting toil were required to cover those thirty terrible miles. And terrible they were, for every foot of them was accomplished at the risk of life to dog and man. A dozen times, Perrault, nosing the way, broke through the ice bridges, being saved by the long pole he carried, which he so held that it fell each time across the hole made by his body. But a cold snap was on, the thermometer registering fifty below zero, and each time he broke through he was compelled for very life to build a fire and dry his garments.

Nothing daunted him. It was because nothing daunted him that he had been choen for government courier. He took all manner of risks, resolutely thrusting his little weazened face into the frost and struggling on from dim dawn to dark. He skirted the frowning shores on rim ice that bent and crackled under foot and upon which they dared not halt. Once, the sled broke through, with Dave and Buck, and they were half-frozen and all but drowned by the time they were dragged out. The usual fire was necessary to save them. They were coated solidly with ice, and the two men kept them on the run around the fire, sweating and thawing, so close that they were singed by the flames.

At another time Spitz went through, dragging the whole team after him up to Buck, who strained backward with all his strength, his fore paws on the slippery edge and the ice quivering and snapping all around. But behind him was Dave, likewise straining backward, and behind the sled was François, pulling till his tendons cracked.

Again the rim ice broke away before and behind, and there was no escape except up the cliff. Perrault scaled it by a miracle, while Francois prayed for just that miracle; and with every thong and sled lashing and the last bit of harness rove into a long rope, the dogs were hoisted, one by one, to the cliff crest. Francois came up last, after the sled and load. Then came the search for a place to descend, which descent was ultimately made by the aid of the the rope, and night found them back on the river with a quarter of a mile to the day's credit.

By the time they made the Hootalinqua and good ice, Buck was played out. The rest of the dogs were in like condition; but Perrault, to make up lost time, pushed them late and early. The first day they covered thirty-five miles to the Big Salmon; the next day thirty-five more to the Little Salmon; the third day forty miles, which brought them well up toward the Five Fingers.

Buck's feet were not so compact and hard as the feet of the huskies. His had softened during the many generations since the day his last wild ancestor was tamed by a cave-dweller or river man. All day long he limped in agony, and camp once made, lay down like a dead dog. hungry as he was, he would not move to receive his ration of fish, which François had to bring to him. Also, the dog-driver rubbed Buck's feet for half an hour each night after supper, and sacrificed the tips of his own moccasins to make four moccasins for Buck. This was a great relief, and Buck caused even the weazened face of Perrault to twist itself into a grin one morning, when François forgot the moccasins and Buck lay on his back, his four feet waving appealingly in the air, and refused to budge without them. Later his feet grew hard to the trail, and the worn-out foot-gear was thrown away.

Buck caused even the weazened face of Perrault
to twist itself into a grin one morning

At the Pelly one morning, as they were harnessing up, Dolly, who had never been conspicuous for anything, went suddenly mad. She announced her condition by a long, heart-breaking wolf howl that sent every dog bristling with fear, then sprang straight for Buck. He had never seen a dog go mad, nor did he have any reason to fear madness; yet he knew that here was horror, and fled away from it in a panic. Straight away he raced, with Dolly, panting and frothing, one leap behind; nor could she gain on him, so great was his terror, nor could he leave her, so great was her madness. He plunged through the wooded breast of the island, flew down to the lower end, crossed a back channel filled with rough ice to another island, gained a third island, curved back to the main river and in desperation started to cross it. And all the time, though he did not look, he could hear her snarling just one leap behind. François called to him a quarter of a mile away and he doubled back, still one leap ahead, gasping painfully for air and putting all his faith in that Francois would save him. The dog-driver held the axe poised in his hand, and as Buck shot past him the axe crashed down upon mad Dolly's head.

Buck staggered over against the sled, exhausted sobbing for breath, helpless. This was Spitz's opportunity. He sprang upon Buck, and twice his teeth sank into his unresisting foe and ripped and tore the flesh to the bone. Then François's lash descended, and Buck had the satisfaction of watching Spitz receive the worst whipping as yet administered to any of the teams.

'One devil, dat Spitz,' remarked Perrault. 'Some dam day heem keel dat Buck.'

'Dat Buck two devils,' was François's rejoinder. 'All de tam I watch dat Buck I know for sure. Lissen: some dam fine day heem get mad lak hell an' den heem chew dat Spitz all up an' spit heem out on de snow. Sure. I know.'

From then on it was war between them. Spitz, as lead-dog and acknowledged master of the team, felt his supremacy threatened by this strange Southland dog. And strange Buck was to him, for of the many Southland dogs he had known, not one had shown up worthily in camp and on trail. They were all too soft, dying under the toil, the frost, and starvation. Buck was the exception. He alone endured and prospered, matching the husky in strength, savagery, and cunning. Then he was a masterful dog, and what made him dangerous was the fact that the club of the man in the red sweater had knocked all blind pluck and rashness out of his desire for mastery. He was pre-eminently cunning; and could bide his time with a patience that was nothing less than primitive.

It was inevitable that the clash for leadership should come. Buck wanted it. He wanted it because it was his nature, because he had been gripped tight by that nameless, incomprehensible pride of the trail and trace – that pride which holds dogs in the toil to the last gasp, which lures them to die joyfully in the harness, and breaks their hearts if they are cut out of the harness. This was the pride of Dave as wheel-dog, so Sol-leks as he pulled with all his strength; the pride that laid hold of them at break of camp, transforming them from sour and sullen brutes into straining, eager, ambitious creatures; the pride that spurred them on all day and dropped them at pitch of camp at night, letting them fall back into gloomy unrest and uncontent. This was the pride that bore up Spitz and made him thrash the sled-dogs who blundered and shirked in the traces or hid away at harness-up time in the morning. Likewise it was this pride that made him fear Buck as a possible lead-dog. And this was Buck's pride, too.

He openly threatened the other's leadership. He came between him and the shirks he should have punished. And he did it deliberately. One night there was a heavy snowfall, and in the morning Pike, the malingerer, did not appear. He was securely hidden in his nest under a foot of snow. Francois called him and sought him in vain. Spitz was wild with wrath. He raged through the camp, smelling and digging in every likely place, snarling so frightfully that Pike heard and shivered in his hiding-place.

But when he was at last unearthed, and Spitz flew at him to punish him, Buck flew, with equal rage, in between. So unexpected was it, and so shrewdly managed, that Spitz was hurled backward and off his feet. Pike, who had been trembling abjectly, took heart at this open mutiny, and sprang upon his overthrown leader. Buck, to whom fair play was a forgotten code, likewise sprang upon Spitz. But François, chuckling at the incident while unswerving in the administration of justice, brought his lash down upon Buck with all his might. This failed to drive Buck from his prostrate rival, and the butt of the whip was brought into play. Half-stunned by the blow, Buck was knocked backward and the lash laid upon him again and again, while Spitz soundly punished the many times offending Pike.

In the days that followed, as Dawson grew closer and closer, Buck still continued to interfere between Spitz and the culprits; but he did it craftily, when François was not around. With the covert mutiny of Buck, a general insubordination sprang up and increased. Dave and Sol-leks were unaffected, but the rest of the team went from bad to worse. Things no longer went right. There was continual bickering and jangling. Trouble was always afoot, and at the bottom of it was Buck. He kept Francois busy, for the dog-driver was in constant apprehension of the life-and-death struggle between the two which he knew must take place sooner or later; and on more than one night the sounds of quarrelling and strife among the other dogs tuned him out of his sleeping robe, fearful that Buck and Spitz were at it.

But the opportunity did not present itself, and they pulled into Dawson one dreary afternoon with the great fight still to come. Here were many men, and countless dogs, and Buck found them all at work. It seemed the ordained order of things that dogs should work. All day they swung up and down the main street in long teams, and in the night their jingling bells still went by. They hauled cabin logs and firewood, freighted up to the mines, and did all manner of work that horses did in the Santa Clara Valley. Here and there Buck met Southland dogs, but in the main they were the wild wolf husky breed. Every night, regularly at night, at twelve, at three, they lifted a nocturnal song, a weird and eerie chant, in which it was Buck's delight to join.

With the aurora borealis flaming coldly overhead, or the stars leaping in the frost dance, and the land numb and frozen under its pall of snow, this song of the huskies might have been the defiance of life, only it was pitched in minor key, with long-drawn wailings and half-

sobs, and was more the pleading of life, the articulate travail of
existence. It was an old song, old as the breed itself – one of the first
songs of the younger world in a day when songs were sad. It was
invested with the woe of unnumbered generations, this plaint by
which Buck was so strangely stirred. When he moaned and sobbed, it
was with the pain of living that was of old the pain of his wild fathers,
and the fear and mystery of the cold and dark that was to them
fear and mystery. And that he should be stirred by it marked
the completeness with which he harked back through the ages of fire
and roof to the raw beginnings of life in the howling ages.

Seven days from the time they pulled into Dawson, they dropped
down the steep band by the Barracks to the Yukon Trail, and pulled
for Dyea and Salt Water. Perrault was carrying despatches if anything
more urgent than those he had brought in; also, the travel pride had
gripped him, and he purposed to make the record trip of the year.
Several things favoured him in this. The week's rest had recuperated
the dogs and put them in thorough trim. The trail they had broken into
the country was packed hard by later journeyers. And further, the
police had arranged in two or three places deposits of grub for dog and
man, and he was travelling light.

They made Sixty Mile, which is a fifty-mile run, on the first day;
and the second day saw them booming up the Yukon well on their way
to Pelly. But such splendid running was achieved not without great
trouble and vexation on the part of François. The insidious revolt led
by Buck had destroyed the solidarity of the team. It no longer was as
one dog leaping in the traces. The encouragement Buck gave the rebels
led them into all kinds of petty misdemeanours. No more was Spitz a
leader greatly to be feared. The old awe departed, and they grew equal
to challenging his authority. Pike robbed him of half a fish one night,
and gulped it down under the protection of Buck. Another night Dub
and Joe fought Spitz and made him forgo the punishment they
deserved. And even Billee, the good-natured, was less good-natured,
and whined not half so placatingly as in former days. Buck never came
near Spitz without snarling and bristling menacingly. In fact, his
conduct approached that of a bully, and he was given to swaggering up

and down before Spitz's very nose.

The breaking down of discipline likewise affected the dogs in their relations with one another. They quarrelled and bickered more than ever among themselves, till at times the camp was a howling bedlam. Dave and Sol-leks alone were unaltered, though they were made irritable by the unending squabbling. François swore strange barbarous oaths, and stamped the snow in futile rage, and tore his hair. His lash was always singing among the dogs, but it was of small avail. Directly his back was turned they were at it again. He backed up Spitz with his whip, while Buck backed up the remainder of the team. François knew he was behind all the trouble, and Buck knew he knew; but Buck was too clever ever again to be caught red-handed. He worked faithfully in the harness, for the toil had become a delight to him; yet it was a greater delight slyly to precipitate a fight amongst his mates and tangle the traces.

At the mouth of the Tahkeena, one night after supper, Dub turned up a snowshoe rabbit, blundered it, and missed. In a second the whole team was in full cry. A hundred yards away was a camp of the Northwest Police, with fifty dogs, huskies all, who joined the chase. The rabbit sped down the river, turned off into a small creek, up the frozen bed of which it held steadily. It ran lightly on the surface of the snow, while the dogs ploughed through by main strength. Buck led the pack, sixty strong, around bend after bend, but he could not gain. He lay down low to the race, whining eagerly, his splendid body flashing forward, leap by leap, in the wan white moonlight. And leap by leap, like some pale frost wraith, the snowshoe rabbit flashed on ahead.

All that stirring of old instincts which at stated periods drives men out from the sounding cities to forest and plain to kill things by chemically propelled leaden pellets, the blood lust, the joy to kill – all this was Buck's, only it was infinitely more intimate. He was ranging at the head of the pack, running the wild thing down, the living meat, to kill with own teeth and wash his muzzle to the eyes in warm blood.

There is an ecstasy that marks the summit of life, and beyond which life cannot rise. And such is the paradox of living, this ecstacy comes when one is most alive, and it comes as a complete forgetfulness that one is alive. This ecstasy, this forgetfulness of living, comes to the artist, caught up and out of himself in a sheet of flame; it comes to the soldier, war-mad on a stricken field and refusing quarter; and it came to Buck, leading the pack, sounding the old wolf-cry, straining after the food that was alive and that fled swiftly before him through the moonlight. He was sounding the deeps of his nature, and of the parts of his nature that were deeper than he, going back into the womb of Time. He was mastered by the sheer surging of life, the tidal wave of being, the perfect joy of each separate muscle, joint, and sinew in that it was everything that was not death, that it was aglow and rampant, expressing itself in movement, flying exultantly under the stars and over the face of dead matter that did not move.

But Spitz, cold and calculating even in his supreme moods, left the pack and cut across a narrow neck of land where the creek made a long bend around. Buck did not know of this, and as he rounded the bend, the frost wraith of a rabbit still flitting before him, he saw another and larger frost wraith leap from the overhanging bank into the immediate path of the rabbit. It was Spitz. The rabbit could not turn, and as the white teeth broke its back in mid air it shrieked as loudly as a stricken man may shriek. At sound of this, the cry of Life plunging down from Life's apex in the grip of Death, the full pack at Buck's heels raised a hell's chorus of delight.

Buck did not cry out. He did not check himself, but drove in upon Spitz, shoulder to shoulder, so hard that he missed the throat. They rolled over and over in the powdery snow. Spitz gained his feet almost as though he had not been overthrown, slashing Buck down the shoulder and leaping clear. Twice his teeth clipped together, like the steel jaws of a trap, as he backed away for betting footing, with lean and lifting lips that writhed and snarled.

In a flash Buck knew it. The time had come. It was to the death. As they circled about, snarling, ears laid back, keenly watchful for the advantage, the scene came to Buck with a sense of familiarity. He seemed to remember it all – the white woods, and earth, and moonlight, and the thrill of battle. Over the whiteness and silence brooded a ghostly calm. There was not the faintest whisper of air –

nothing moved, not a leaf quivered, the visible breaths of the dogs rising slowly and lingering in the frosty air. They had made short work of the snow-shoe rabbit, these dogs that were ill-tamed wolves; and they were now drawn up in an expectant circle. They, too, were silent, their eyes only gleaming and their breaths drifting slowly upward. To Buck it was nothing new or strange, this scene of old time. It was as though it had always been the wonted way of things.

Spitz was a practised fighter. From Spitzbergen through the Arctic, and across Canada and the Barrens, he had held his own with all manner of dogs and achieved to mastery over them. Bitter rage was his, but never blind rage. In passion to rend and destroy, he never forgot that his enemy was in like passion to rend and destroy. He never rushed till he was prepared to receive a rush; never attacked till he had first defended that attack.

In vain Buck strove to sink his teeth in the neck of the big white dog. Wherever his fangs struck for the softer flesh, they were countered by the fangs of Spitz. Fang clashed fang, and lips were cut and bleeding, but Buck could not penetrate his enemy's guard. Then he warmed up and enveloped Spitz in a whirlwind of rushes. Time and time again he tried for the snow-white throat, where life bubbled near to the surface, and each time and every time Spitz slashed him and got away. Then Buck took to rushing, as though for the throat, when, suddenly drawing back his head and curving in from the side, he would drive his shoulder at the shoulder of Spitz, as a ram by which to overthrow him. But instead, Buck's shoulder was slashed down each time as Spitz leaped lightly away.

Spitz was untouched, while Buck was streaming with blood and panting hard. The fight was growing desperate. And all the while the silent and wolfish circle waited to finish off whichever dog went down. As Buck grew winded, Spitz took to rushing, and he kept him staggering for footing. Once Buck went over, and the whole circle of sixty dogs started up; but he recovered himself, almost in mid air, and the circle sank down again and waited.

But Buck possessed a quality that made for greatness – imagination. He fought by instinct, but he could fight by head as well. He rushed, as though attempting the old shoulder trick, but at the last instant swept low to the snow and in. His teeth closed on Spitz's left fore leg. There was a crunch of breaking bone, and the white dog faced him on three legs. Thrice he tried to knock him over, then repeated the trick and broke the right fore leg. Despite the pain and helplessness, Spitz struggled madly to keep up. He saw the silent circle, with gleaming eyes, lolling tongues, and silvery breaths drifting upward, closing in upon him as he had seen similar circles close in upon beaten antagonists in the past. Only this time he was the one who was beaten.

There was no hope for him. Buck was inexorable. Mercy was a thing reserved for gentler climes. He manœuvred for the final rush. The circle had tightened till he could feel the breaths of the huskies on his flanks. He could see them, beyond Spitz and to either side, half crouching for the spring, their eyes fixed upon him. A pause seemed to fall. Every animal was motionless as though turned to stone. Only Spitz quivered and bristled as he staggered back and forth, snarling with horrible menace, as though to frighten off impending death. Then Buck sprang in and out; but while he was in, shoulder had at last squarely met shoulder. The dark circle became a dot on the moon-flooded snow as Spitz disappeared from view. Buck stood and looked on, the successful champion, the dominant primordial beast who had made his kill and found it good.

4   Who Has Won to Mastership

'Eh? Wot I say? I spik true w'en I say dat Buck two devils.'

This was François's speech next morning when he discovered Spitz missing and Buck covered with wounds. He drew him to the fire and by its light pointed them out.

'Dat Spitz fight lak hell,' said Perrault, as he surveyed the gaping rips and cuts.

'An' dat Buck fight lak two hells,' was Francois's answer. 'An' now we make good time. No more Spitz, no more trouble, sure.'

While Perrault packed the camp outfit and loaded the sled, the dog-driver proceeded to harness the dogs. Buck trotted up to the place Spitz would have occupied as leader; but François, not noticing him, brought Sol-leks to the coveted position. In his judgment, Sol-leks was the best lead-dog left. Buck spang upon Sol-leks in a fury, driving him back and standing in his place.

'Eh? eh?' François cried, slapping his thighs gleefully. 'Look at dat Buck. Heem keel dat Spitz, hee, t'ink to take de job.'

'Go 'way, Chook!' he cried, but Buck refused to budge.

He took Buck by the scruff of the neck, and though the dog growled threateningly, dragged him to one side and replaced Sol-leks. The old dog did not like it, and showed plainly that he was afraid of Buck. François was obdurate, but when he turned his back Buck again displaced Sol-leks, who was not at all unwilling to go.

François was angry. 'Now, by Gar, I feex you!' he cried, coming back with a heavy club in his hand.

Buck remembered the man in the red sweater, and retreated slowly; nor did he attempt to charge in when Sol-leks was once more brought forward. But he circled just beyond the range of the club, snarling with bitterness and rage; and while he circled he watched the club so as to dodge it if thrown by Francois, for he was become wise in the way of clubs.

The driver went about his work, and he called to Buck he was ready to put him in his old place in front of Dave. Buck retreated two or three steps. Francois followed him up, whereupon he again retreated. After some time of this, François threw down his club, thinking that Buck feared a thrashing. But Buck was in open revolt. He wanted not to escape a clubbing but to have the leadership. It was his by right. He had earned it, and he would not be content with less.

Perrault took a hand. Between them they ran him about for the better part of an hour. They threw clubs at him. He dodged. They cursed him, and his father and mothers before him, and all his seed to come after him down to the remotest generation, and every hair on his body and drop of blood in his veins; and he answered curse with snarl and kept out of their reach. He did not try to run away, but retreated around and around the camp, advertising plainly that when his desire was met, he would come in and be good.

François sat down and scratched his head. Perrault looked at his watch and swore. Time was flying, and they should have been on the trail an hour gone. François scratched his head again. He shook it and grinned sheepishly at the courier, who shrugged his shoulders in sign that they were beaten. Then François went up to where Sol-leks stood and called to Buck. Buck laughed, as dogs laugh, yet kept his distance. Francois unfastened Sol-leks's traces and put him back in his old place. The team stood harnessed to the sled in an unbroken line, ready for the trail. There was no place for Buck save at the front. Once more Francois called, and once more Buck laughed and kept away.

'T'row down de club,' Perrault commanded.

François complied, whereupon Buck trotted in, laughing triumphantly, and swung around into position at the head of the team. His traces were fastened, the sled broken out, and with both men running they dashed out on to the river trail.

Highly as the dog-driver had forevalued Buck, with his two devils, he found, while the day was yet young, that he had undervalued. At a

*Buck trotted in laughing triumphantly, and swung round
into position at the head of the team*

bound Buck took up the duties of leadership; and where judgment was required, and quick thinking and quick acting, he showed himself the superior even of Spitz, of whom François had never seen an equal.

But it was in giving the law and making his mates live up to it, that Buck excelled. Dave and Sol-leks did not mind the change in leadership. It was none of their business. Their business was to toil, and toil mightily, in the traces. So long as that were not interfered with, they did not care what happened. Billee, the good-natured, could lead for all they cared so long as he kept order. The rest of the team, however, had grown unruly during the last days of Spitz, and their surprise was great now that Buck proceeded to lick them into shape.

Pike, who pulled at Buck's heels, and who never put an ounce more of his weight against the breast-band that he was compelled to do, was swiftly and repeatedly shaken for loafing; and ere the first day was done he was pulling more than ever before in his life. The first night in camp, Joe, the sour one, was punished roundly – a thing that Spitz had never succeeded in doing. Buck simply smothered him by virtue of superior weight, and cut him up till he ceased snapping and began to whine for mercy.

The general tone of the team picked up immediately. It recovered its old-time solidarity, and once more the dogs leaped as one dog in the traces. At the Rink Rapids two native huskies, Teek and Koona, were added; and the celerity with which Buck broke them in took away François's breath.

'Nevaire such a dog as dat Buck!' he cried. 'No, nevaire! Heem worth one t'ousan' dollair, by Gar! Eh? Wot you say, Perrault?'

And Perrault nodded. He was ahead of the record then, and gaining day by day. The trail was in excellent condition, well packed and hard, and there was no new-fallen snow with which to contend. It was not too cold. The temperature dropped to fifty below zero and remained there the whole trip. The men rode and ran by turn, and the dogs were kept on the jump, with but infrequent stoppages.

The Thirty Mile River was comparatively coated with ice, and they covered in one day going out what had taken them ten days coming in. In one run they made a sixty-mile dash from the foot of

Lake Le Barge to the White Horse Rapids. Across Marsh, Tagish, and Bennett (seventy miles of lakes), they flew so fast that the man whose turn it was to run towed behind the sled at the end of a rope. And on the last night of the second week they topped White Pass and dropped down the sea slope with the lights of Skaguay and of the shipping at their feet.

It was a record run. Each day for fourteen days they had averaged forty miles. For three days Perrault and François threw chests up and down the main street of Skaguay and were deluged with invitations to drink, while the team was the constant centre of a worshipful crowd of dog-buster and mushers. Then three or four western bad men aspired to clean out the town, were riddled like pepper-boxes for their pains, and public interest turned to other idols. Next came official orders. François called Buck to him, threw his arms around him, wept over him. And that was the last of Francois and Perrault. Like other men, they passed out of Buck's life for good.

A Scotch half-breed took charge of him and his mates, and in company with a dozen other dog-teams he started back over the weary trail to Dawson. It was no light running now, nor record time, but heavy toil each day, with a heavy load behind; for this was the mail train, carrying word from the world to the men who sought gold under the shadow of the Pole.

Buck did not like it, but he bore up well to the work, taking pride in it after the manner of Dave and Sol-leks, and seeing his mates, whether they prided in it or not, did their fair share. It was a montonous life, operating with machine-like regularity. One day was very like another. At a certain time each morning the cooks turned out, fires were built, and breakfast was eaten. Then, while some broke camp, others harnessed the dogs, and they were under way an hour or so before the darkness fell which gave warning of dawn. At night, camp was made. Some pitched the flies, others cut firewood and pine boughs for the beds, and still others carried water or ice for the cooks. Also, the dogs were fed. To them, this was the one feature of the day, though it was good to loaf around, after the fish was eaten, for an hour or so with the other dogs, of which there were fivescore and odd. There were fierce fighters among them, but three battles with the fiercest brought Buck to mastery, so that when he bristled and showed his teeth they got out of the way.

Best of all, perhaps he loved to lie near the fire, hind legs crouched under him, fore legs stretched out in front, head raised, and eyes blinking dreamily at the flames. Sometimes he thought of Judge Miller's big house in the sun-kissed Santa Clara Valley, and of the cement swimming-tank, and Ysabel, the Mexican hairless, and Toots, the Japanese pug; but oftener he remembered the man in the red sweater, the death of Curly, the great fight with Spitz, and the good things he had eaten or would like to eat. He was not homesick. The Sunland was very dim and distant, and such memories had no power over him. Far more potent were the memories of his heredity that gave things he had never seen before a seeming familiarity; the instincts (which were but the memories of his ancestors become habits) which had lapsed in later days, and still later, in him, quickened and become alive again.

Sometimes as he crouched there, blinking dreamily at the flames, it seemed that the flames were of another fire, and that as he crouched by this other fire he saw another and different man from the half-breed cook before him. This other man was shorter of leg and longer of arm, with muscles that were stringy and knotty rather than rounded and swelling. The hair of this man was long and matted, and his head slanted back under it from the eyes. He uttered strange sounds, and seemed very much afraid of the darkness, into which he peered continually, clutching in his hand, which hung midway between knee and foot, a stick with a heavy stone made fast to the end. He was all but naked, a ragged and fire-scorched skin hanging part way down his back, but on his body there was much hair. In some places, across the chest and shoulders and down the outside of the arms and thighs, it was matted into almost a thick fur. He did not stand erect, but with trunk inclined forward from the hips, on legs that bent at the knees. About his body there was a peculiar springiness, or resiliency, almost catlike, and quick alertness as of one who lived in perpetual fear of things seen and unseen.

At other times this hairy man squatted by the fire with head between his legs and slept. On such occasions his elbows were on his knees, his hands clasped above his head as though to shed rain by the hairy arms. And beyond that fire, in the circling darkness, Buck could see many gleaming coals, two by two, always two by two, which he knew to be the eyes of great beasts of prey. And he could hear the crashing of their bodies through the undergrowth, and the noises they made in the night. And dreaming there by the Yukon bank, with lazy eyes blinking at the fire, these sounds and sights of another world would make the hair to rise along his back and stand on end across his shoulders and up his neck, till he whimpered low and suppressedly, or growled softly, and the half-breed cook shouted at him, 'Hey, you Buck, wake up!' Whereupon the other world would vanish and the real world come into his eyes, and he would get up and yawn and stretch as though he had been asleep.

It was a hard trip, with the mail behind them, and the heavy work wore them down. They were short of weight and in poor condition when they made Dawson, and should have had a ten days' or a week's rest at least. But in two days' time they dropped down the Yukon bank from the Barracks, loaded with letters for the outside. The dogs were tired, the drivers grumbling, and, to make matters worse, it snowed every day. This meant a soft trail, greater friction on the runners, and heavier pulling for the dogs; yet the drivers were fair through it all, and did their best for the animals.

Each night the dogs were attended to first. They ate before the drivers ate, and no man sought his sleeping robe till he had seen to the feet of the dogs he drove. Still, their strength went down. Since the beginning of the winter they had travelled eighteen hundred miles, dragging sleds the whole weary distance; and eighteen hundred miles will tell upon life of the toughest. Buck stood it, keeping his mates up to their work and maintaining discipline, though he, too, was very tired. Billee cried and whimpered regularly in his sleep each night. Joe was sourer than ever, and Sol-leks was unapproachable, blind side or other side.

But it was Dave who suffered most of all. Something had gone wrong with him. He become more morose and irritable, and when

camp was pitched at once made his nest, where his driver fed him.
Once out of the harness and down, he did not get on his feet again till
harness-up time in the morning. Sometimes, in the traces, when
jerked by a sudden stoppage of the sled, or by straining to start it, he
would cry out with pain. The driver examined him, but could find
nothing. All the drivers became interested in his case. They talked it
over at meal-time, and over their last pipes before going to bed, and
one night they held a consultation. He was brought from his nest to the
fire and was pressed and prodded till he cried out many times.
Something was wrong inside, but they could locate no broken bones,
could not make it out.

By the time Cassiar Bar was reached, he was so weak that he was
falling repeatedly in the traces. The Scotch half-breed called a halt and
took him out of the team, making the next dog, Sol-leks, fast to the
sled. His intention was to rest Dave, letting him run free behind the
sled. Sick as he was, Dave resented being taken out, grunting and
growling while the traces were unfastened, and whimpering broken-
heartedly when he saw Sol-lek in the position he had held and served
so long. For the pride of trace and trail was his, and, sick unto his
death, he could not bear that another dog should do his work.

When the sled started, he floundered in the soft snow alongside the
beaten trail, attacking Sol-leks with his teeth, rushing against him and
trying to thrust him off into the soft snow on the other side, striving to
leap inside his traces and get between him and the sled, and all the
while whining and yelping and crying with grief and pain. The half-
breed tried to drive him away with the whip; but he paid no heed to the
stinging lash, and the man had not the heart to strike harder. Dave
refused to run quietly on the trail behind the sled, where the going
was easy, but continued to flounder alongside in the soft snow, where
the going was most difficult, till exhausted. Then he fell, and lay
where he fell, howling lugubriously as the long train sleds churned
by.

With the last remnant of his strength he managed to stagger along
behind till the train made another stop, when he floundered past the
sleds to his own, where he stood alongside Sol-leks. His driver lingered

a moment to get a light for his pipe from the man behind. Then he returned and started his dogs. They swung out on the trail with remarkable lack of exertion, turned their heads uneasily, and stopped in surprise. The driver was surprised, too; the sled had not moved. He called his comrades to witness the sight. Dave had bitten through both of Sol-leks's traces, and was standing directly in front of the sled in his proper place.

He pleaded with his eyes to remain there. The driver was perplexed. His comrades talked of how a dog could break its heart through being denied the work that killed it, and recalled instances they had known, where dogs, too old for the toil, or injured, had died because they were cut out of the traces. Also, they held it a mercy, since Dave was to die anyway, that he should die in the traces, heart-easy and content. So he was harnessed in again, and proudly he pulled as of old, though more than once he cried out involuntarily from the bite of his inward hurt. Several times he fell down and was dragged in the traces, and once the sled ran upon him so that he limped thereafter in one of his hind legs.

But he held out till camp was reached, when his driver made a place for him by the fire. Morning found him too weak to travel. At harness-up time he tried to crawl to his driver. By convulsive efforts he got on his feet, staggered, and fell. Then he wormed his way forward slowly toward where the harnesses were being put on his mates. He would advance his fore legs and drag up his body with a sort of hitching movement, when he would advance his fore legs and hitch ahead again for a few more inches. His strength left him, and the last his mates saw of him he lay gasping in the snow and yearning toward them. But they could hear him mournfully howling, till they passed out of sight behind a belt of river timber.

Here the train was halted. The Scotch half-breed slowly retraced his steps to the camp they had left. The men ceased talking. A revolver-shot rang out. The man came back hurriedly. The whips snapped, the bells tinkled merrily, the sleds churned along the trail; but Buck knew, and every dog knew, what had taken place behind the belt of river trees.

5   The Toil of Trace and Trail

Thirty days from the time it left Dawson, the Salt Water Mail, with
Buck and his mates at the fore, arrived at Skaguay. They were in a
wretched state, worn out and worn down. Buck's one hundred and
forty pounds had dwindled to one hundred and fifteen. The rest of his
mates, though lighter dogs, had relatively lost more weight than he.
Pike, the malingerer, who, in his lifetime of deceit, had often
successfully feigned a hurt leg, was now limping in earnest. Sol-leks
was limping, and Dub was suffering from a wrenched shoulder-blade.

They were all terribly footsore. No spring or rebound was left in
them. Their feet fell heavily on the trail, jarring their bodies and
doubling the fatigue of a day's travel. There was nothing the matter
with them except that they were dead tired. It was not the dead-
tiredness that comes through brief and excessive effort, from which
recovery is a matter of hours; but it was the dead-tiredness that comes
through the slow and prolonged strength drainage of months of toil.
There was no power of recuperation left, no reserve strength to call
upon. It had been all used, the last least bit of it. Every muscle, every
fibre, every cell, was tired, dead tired. And there was reason for it. In
less than five months they had travelled twenty-five hundred miles,
during the last eighteen hundred of which they had had but five days'
rest. When they arrived at Skaguay they were apparently on their last
legs. They could barely keep the traces taut, and on the down grades
just managed to keep out of the way of the sled.

'Mush on, poor sore feets,' the driver encouraged them as they
tottered down the main street of Skaguay. 'Dis is de las'. Den we get

one long res'. Eh? For sure. One bully long res'.'

The drivers confidently expected a long stopover. Themselves, they had covered twelve hundred miles with two days' rest, and in the nature of reason and common justice they deserved an interval of loafing. But so many were the men who had rushed into the Klondyke, and so many were the sweethearts, wives, and kin that had not rushed in, that the congested mail was taking on Alpine proportions; also there were official orders. Fresh batches of Hudson Bay dogs were to take the places of those worthless for the trail. The worthless ones were to be got rid of, and since dogs count for little against dollars, they were to be sold.

Three days passed, by which time Buck and his mates found how really tired and weak they were. Then, on the morning of the fourth day, two men from the States came along and bought them, harness and all, for a song. The men addressed each other as 'Hal' and 'Charles'. Charles was a middle-aged, lightish-coloured man, with weak and watery eyes and a moustache that twisted fiercely and vigorously up, giving the lie to the limply drooping lip it concealed. Hal was a youngster of nineteen or twenty, with a big Colt's revolver and a hunting-knife strapped about him on a belt that fairly bristled with cartridges. This belt was the most salient thing about him. It advertised his callowness – a callowness sheer and unutterable. Both men were manifestly out of place, and why such as they should adventure the North is part of the mystery of things that passes understanding.

Buck heard the chaffering, saw the money pass between the man and the Government agent, and knew that the Scotch half-breed and the mail-train drivers were passing out of his life on the heels of Perrault and François and the others who had gone before. When driven with his mates to the new owners' camp, Buck saw a slipshod and slovenly affair, tent half stretched, dishes unwashed, everything in disorder; also, he saw a woman. 'Mercedes' the men called her. She was Charles's wife and Hal's sister – a nice family party.

Buck watched them apprehensively as they proceeded to take down the tent and load the sled. There was a great deal of effort about their manner, but no business-like method. The tent was rolled into an awkward bundle three times as large as it should have been. The tin dishes were packed away unwashed. Mercedes continually fluttered in the way of her men and kept up an unbroken chattering of remonstrance and advice. When they put a clothes-sack on the front of the sled, she suggested it should go on the back; and when they had put it on the back, and covered it over with a couple of other bundles, she discovered overlooked articles which could abide nowhere else but in that sack, and they unloaded again.

Three men from a neighbouring tent came out and looked on, grinning and winking at one another.

'You've got a right smart load as it is,' said one of them; 'and it's not me should tell you your business, but I wouldn't tote that tent along if I was you.'

'Undreamed of!' cried Mercedes, throwing up her hands in dainty dismay. 'However in the world could I manage without a tent?'

'It's springtime, and you won't get any more cold weather,' the man replied.

She shook her head decidedly, and Charles and Hal put the last odds and ends on top of the mountainous load.

'Think it'll ride?' one of the men asked.

'Why shouldn't it?' Charles demanded rather shortly.

'Oh, that's all right, that's all right,' the man hastened meekly to say. 'I was just a-wonderin', that is all. It seemed a mite top-heavy.'

Charles turned his back and drew the lashing down as well as he could, which was not in the least well.

'An' of course the dogs can hike along all day with that contraption behind them,' affirmed a second of the men.

'Certainly,' said Hal, with freezing politeness, taking hold of the gee-pole with one hand and swinging his whip from the other. 'Mush!' he shouted. 'Mush on there!'

The dogs sprang against the breast-bands, strained hard for a few moments, then relaxed. They were unable to move the sled.

'The lazy brutes, I'll show them,' he cried, preparing to lash out at them with the whip.

But Mercedes interfered, crying, 'Oh, Hal, you musn't,' as she caught hold of the whip and wrenched it from him. 'The poor dears! Now you must promise you won't be harsh with them for the rest of the trip, or I won't go a step.'

'Precious lot you know about dogs,' her brother sneered; 'and I wich you'd leave me alone. They're lazy, I tell you, and you've got to whip them to get anything out of them. That's their way. You ask any one. Ask one of those men.'

Mercedes looked at them imploringly, untold repugnance at sight of pain written in her pretty face.

'They're weak as water, if you want to know,' came the reply from one of the men. 'Plum tuckered out, that's what's the matter. They need a rest.'

'Rest be blanked,' said Hal, with his beardless lips; and Mercedes said, 'Oh!' in pain and sorrow at the oath.

But she was a clannish creature, and rushed at once to the defence of her brother. 'Never mind that man,' she said pointedly. 'You're driving our dogs, and you do what you think best with them.'

Again Hal's whip fell upon the dogs. They threw themselves against the breast-bands, dug their feet into the packed snow, got down low to it, and put forth all their strength. The sled held as though it were an anchor. After two efforts, they stood still, panting. The whip was whistling savagely, when once more Mercedes interfered. She dropped on her knees before Buck, with tears in her eyes, and put her arms around his neck.

'You poor, poor dears,' she cried sympathetically, 'why don't you pull hard? – then you wouldn't be whipped.' Buck did not like her, but he was feeling too miserable to resist her, taking it as part of the day's miserable work.

One of the onlookers, who had been clenching his teeth to suppress hot speech, now spoke up:

'It's not that I care a whoop what becomes of you, but for the dogs' sakes I just want to tell you, you can help them a mighty lot by breaking out that sled. The runners are froze fast. Throw your weight against the gee-pole, right and left, and break it out.'

A third time the attempt was made, but this time, following the advice, Hal broke out the runners which had been frozen to the snow. The overloaded and unwieldy sled forged ahead. Buck and his mates struggled frantically under the rain of blows. A hundred yards ahead the path turned and sloped steeply into the main street. It would have required an experienced man to keep the top-heavy sled upright, and Hal was not such a man. As they swung on the turn the sled went over, spilling half its load through the loose lashings. The dogs never stopped. The lightened sled bounded on its side behind them. They were angry because of the ill treatment they had received and the unjust load. Buck was raging. He broke into a run, the team following his lead. Hal cried 'Whoa! whoa!' but they gave no heed. He tripped and was pulled off his feet. The capsized sled ground over him, and the dogs dashed on up the street, adding to the gaiety of Skaguay as they scattered the remainder of the outfit along its chief thoroughfare.

Kind-hearted citizens caught the dogs and gathered up the scattered belongings. Also, they gave advice. Half the load and twice the dogs, if they ever expected to reach Dawson, was what was said. Hal and his sister and brother-in-law listened unwillingly, pitched tent, and overhauled the outfit. Canned goods were turned out that made men laugh, for canned goods on the Long Trail is a thing to dream about. 'Blankets for a hotel,' quoth one of the men who laughed and helped. 'Half as many is too much; get rid of them. Throw away that tent, and all those dishes – who's going to wash them, anyway? Good Lord, do you think you're travelling on a Pullman?'

And so it went, the inexorable elimination of the superfluous. Mercedes cried when her clothes-bags were dumped on the ground and article after article was thrown out. She cried in general, and she cried in particular over each discarded thing. She clasped hands about knees, rocking back and forth broken-heartedly. She averred she would not go an inch, not for a dozen Charleses. She appealed to everybody and to everything, finally wiping her eyes and proceeding to cast out even articles of apparel that were imperative necessities. And in her zeal, when she had finished with her own, she attacked the belongings of her men and went through them like a tornado.

This accomplished, the outfit, though cut in half, was still a formidable bulk. Charles and Hal went out in the evening and bought six Outside dogs. These, added to the six of the original team, and Teek and Koona, the huskies obtained at the Rink Rapids on the record trip, brought the team up to fourteen. But the Outside dogs, though practically broken in since their landing, did not amount to much. Three were short-haired pointers, one was a Newfoundland, and the other two were mongrels of indeterminate breed. They did not seem to know anything, these newcomers. Buck and his comrades looked upon them with disgust, and though he speedily taught them their places and what not to do, he could not teach them what to do. They did not take kindly to trace and trail. With the exception of the two mongrels, they were bewildered and spirit-broken by the strange savage environment in which they found themselves and by the ill-treatment they had received. The two mongrels were without spirit at all; bones were the only things breakable about them.

With the newcomers hopeless and forlorn, and the old team worn out by twenty-five hundred miles of continuous trail, the outlook was anything but bright. The two men, however, were quite cheerful. And they were proud, too. They were doing the thing in style, with fourteen dogs. They had seen other sleds depart over the Pass for Dawson, or come in from Dawson, but never had they seen a sled with so many as fourteen dogs. In the nature of Arctic travel there was a reason why fourteen dogs should not drag one sled, and that was that one sled could not carry the food for fourteen dogs. But Charles and Hal did not know this. They had worked the trip out with a pencil, so much to a dog, so many dogs, so many days, Q.E.D. Mercedes looked over their shoulders and nodded comprehensively, it was all so very simple.

Late next morning Buck led the long team up the street. There was nothing lively about it, no snap or go in him and his fellows. They were starting dead weary. Four times he had covered the distance between Salt Water and Dawson, and the knowledge that, jaded and tired, he was facing the same trail once more, made him bitter. His heart was not in the work, nor was the heart of any dog. The Outsides were timid and frightened, the Insides without confidence in their masters.

Buck felt vaguely that there was no depending upon these two men and the woman. They did not know how to do anything, and as the days went by it became apparent that they could not learn. They were slack in all things, without order or discipline. It took them half the night to pitch a slovenly camp, and half the morning to break that camp and get the sled loaded in fashion so slovenly that for the rest of the day they were occupied in stopping and rearranging the load. Some days they did not make ten miles. On other days they were unable to get started at all. And on no day did they succeed in making more than half the distance used by the men as a basis in their dog-food computation.

It was inevitable that they should go short on dog-food. But they hastened it by over-feeding, bringing the day nearer when under-feeding would commence. The Outside dogs, whose digestions had not been trained by chronic famine to make the most of little, had voracious appetites. And when, in addition to this, the worn-out huskies pulled weakly, Hal decided that the orthodox ration was too small. He doubled it. And to cap it all, when Mercedes, with tears in her pretty eyes and a quaver in her throat, could not cajole him into giving the dogs still more, she stole from the fish-sacks and fed them slyly. But it was not food that Buck and the huskies needed, but rest. And though they were making poor time, the heavy load they dragged sapped their strength severely.

Then came the under-feeding. Hal awoke one day to the fact that his dog-food was half gone and the distance only quarter covered; further, that for love or money no additional dog-food was to be obtained. So he cut down even the orthodox ration and tried to increase the day's travel. His sister and brother-in-law seconded him; but they were frustrated by their heavy outfit and their own incompetence. It was a simple matter to give the dogs less food; but it was impossible to make the dogs travel faster, while their own inability to get under way earlier in the morning prevented them from travelling longer hours. Not only did they not know how to work dogs, but they did not know how to work themselves.

The first to go was Dub. Poor blundering thief that he was, always getting caught and punished, he had none the less been a faithful worker. His wrenched shoulderblade, untreated and unrested, went from bad to worse, till finally Hal shot him with the big Colt's revolver. It is a saying of the country that an Outside dog starves to death on the ration of the husky, so the six Outside dogs under Buck could do no less than die on half the ration of the husky. The Newfoundland went first, followed by the three short-haired pointers, the two mongrels hanging more grittily on to life, but going in the end.

By this time all the amenities and gentlenesses of the Southland had fallen away from the three people. Shorn of its glamour and romance, Arctic travel became to them a reality too harsh for their manhood and womanhood. Mercedes ceased weeping over the dogs, being too occupied with weeping over herself and with quarrelling with her husband and brother. To quarrel was the one thing they were never too weary to do. Their irritability arose out of their misery, increased with it, doubled upon it, outdistanced it. The wonderful patience of the trail which comes to men who toil hard and suffer sore, and remain sweet of speech and kindly, did not come to these two men and the woman. They had no inkling of such a patience. They were stiff and in pain; their muscles ached, their bones ached, their very hearts ached; and because of this they became sharp of speech, and hard words were first on their lips in the morning and last at night.

Charles and Hal wrangled whenever Mercedes gave them a chance. It was the cherished belief of each that he did more than his share of the work, and neither forbore to speak his belief at every opportunity. Sometimes Mercedes sided with her husband, sometimes with her brother. The result was a beautiful and unending family quarrel. Starting from a dispute as to which should chop a few sticks for the fire (a dispute which concerned only Charles and Hal), presently would be lugged in the rest of the family, fathers, mothers, uncles, cousins, people thousands of miles away and some of them dead. That Hal's views on art, or the sort of society plays his mother's brother wrote, should have anything to do with the chopping of a few sticks of firewood, passes comprehension; nevertheless the quarrel was as likely to tend in that direction as in the direction of Charles's political prejudices. And that Charles's sister's tale-bearing tongue should be relevant to the building of a Yukon fire, was apparent only to Mercedes, who disburdened herself of copious opinions upon that topic, and incidentally upon a few other traits unpleasantly peculiar to her husband's family. In the meantime the fire remained unbuilt, the camp half pitched, and the dogs unfed.

Mercedes nursed a special grievance – the grievance of her sex. She was pretty and soft, and had been chivalrously treated all her days. But the present treatment by her husband and brother was everything save chivalrous. It was her custom to be helpless. They complained. Upon which impeachment of what to her was her most essential sex-prerogative, she made their lives unendurable. She no longer considered the dogs, and because she was sore and tired, she persisted in riding on the sled. She was pretty and soft, but she weighed one hundred and twenty pounds – a lusty last straw to the load dragged by the weak and starving animals. She rode for days, till they fell in the traces and the sled stood still. Charles and Hal begged her to get off and walk, pleaded with her, entreated, the while she wept and importuned Heaven with a recital of their brutality.

On one occasion they took her off the sled by main strength. They never did it again. She let her legs go limp like a spoiled child, and sat down on the trail. They went on their way, but she did not move. After they had travelled three miles they unloaded the sled, came back for her, and by main strength put her on the sled again.

In the excess of their own misery they were callous to the suffering of their animals. Hal's theory, which he practised on others, was that one must get hardened. He had started out preaching it to his sister and brother-in-law. Failing there, he hammered it into the dogs with a club. At the Five Fingers the dog-food gave out, and a toothless old squaw offered to trade them a few pounds of frozen horse-hide for the Colt's revolver that kept the big hunting-knife company at Hal's hip. A poor substitute for food was this hide, just as it had been stripped from the starved horses of the cattlemen six months back. In its frozen state it was more like strips of galvanised iron, and when a dog wrestled it into his stomach it thawed into thin and innutritious leathery strings and into a mass of short hair, irritating and indigestible. And through it all Buck staggered along at the head of the team as in a nightmare. He pulled when he could; when he could no longer pull, he fell down and remained till blows from whip or club drove him to his feet again. All the stiffness and gloss had gone out of his beautiful furry coat. The hair hung down, limp and draggled, or matted with dried blood where Hal's club had bruised him. His muscles had wasted away to knotty strings, and the flesh pads had disappeared, so that each rib and every bone in his frame were outlined cleanly through the loose hide that was wrinkled in folds of emptiness. It was heartbreaking, only Buck's heart was unbreakable. The man in the red sweater had proved that.

As it was with Buck, so was it with his mates. They were perambulating skeletons. There were seven all together, including him. In their very great misery they had become insensible to the bite of the lash or the bruise of the club. The pain of the beating was dull and distant, just as the things their eyes saw and their ears heard seemed dull and distant. They were not half living, or quarter living. They were simply so many bags of bones in which sparks of life fluttered faintly. When a halt was made, they dropped down in the traces like dead dogs, and the spark dimmed and paled and seemed to go out. And when the club or whip fell upon them, the spark fluttered feebly up, and they tottered to their feet and staggered on.

There came a day when Billee, the good-natured, fell and could not rise. Hal had traded off his revolver, so he took the axe and knocked Billee on the head as he lay in the traces, then cut the carcass out of the harness and dragged it to one side. Buck saw, and his mates saw, and they knew that this thing was very close to them. On the next day Koona went, and but five of them remained: Joe, too far gone to be malignant; Pike, crippled and limping, only half conscious and not conscious enough longer to malinger; Sol-leks, the one-eyed, still faithful to the toil of trace and trail, and mournful in that he had so little strength with which to pull; Teek, who had not travelled so far that winter and who was now beaten more than the others because he was fresher; and Buck, still at the head of the team, but no longer enforcing discipline or striving to enforce it, blind with weakness half the time and keeping the trail by the loom of it and by the dim feel of his feet.

It was beautiful spring weather, but neither dogs nor humans were aware of it. Each day the sun rose earlier and set later. It was dawn by three in the morning, and twilight lingered till nine at night. The whole long day was a blaze of sunshine. The ghostly winter silence had given way to the great spring murmur of awakening life. The murmur arose from all the land, fraught with the joy of living. It came from the things that lived and moved again, things which had been as dead and which had not moved during the long months of frost. The sap was rising in the pines. The willows and aspens were bursting out in young buds. Shrubs and vines were putting on fresh garbs of green. Crickets sang in the nights, and in the days all manner of creeping, crawling things rustled forth into the sun. Partridges and woodpeckers were booming and knocking in the forest. Squirrels were chattering, birds singing, and overhead honked the wild-fowl driving up from the south in cunning wedges that split the air.

From every hill slope came the trickle of running water, the music of unseen fountains. All things were thawing, bending, snapping. The Yukon was straining to break loose the ice that bound it down. It ate away from beneath; the sun ate from above. Air-holes formed, fissures sprang and spread apart, while thin section of ice fell through bodily into the river. And amid all this bursting, rending, throbbing of awakening life, under the blazing sun and through the soft-sighing breezes, like wayfarers to death, staggered the two men, the woman, and the huskies.

With the dogs falling, Mercedes weeping and riding, Hal swearing innocuously, and Charles's eyes wistfully watering, they staggered into John Thornton's camp at the mouth of White River. When they halted, the dogs dropped down as though they had all been struck dead. Mercedes dried her eyes and looked at John Thorton. Charles sat down on a log to rest. He sat down very slowly and painstakingly what of his great stiffness. Hal did the talking. John Thornton was whittling the last touches of an axe-handle he had made from a stick of birch. He whittled and listened, gave monosyllabic replies, and, when it was asked, terse advice. He knew the breed, and he gave his advice in the certainty that it would not be followed.

'They told us up above that the bottom was dropping out of the trail and that the best thing for us to do was to lay over,' Hal said in response to Thornton's warning to take no more chances on the rotten ice. 'They told us we couldn't make White River, and here we are.' This last with a sneering ring of triumph in it.

'And they told you true,' John Thornton answered. 'The bottom's likely to drop out at any moment. Only fools, with the blind luck of fools, could have made it. I tell you straight, I wouldn't risk my carcass on that ice for all the gold in Alaska.'

'That's because you're not a fool, I suppose,' said Hal. 'All the same, we'll go on to Dawson.' He uncoiled his whip. 'Get up there, Buck! Hi! Get up there! Mush on!'

Thornton went on whittling. It was idle, he knew, to get between a fool and his folly; while two or three fools more or less would not alter the scheme of things.

But the team did not get up at the command. It had long since passed into the stage where blows were required to rouse it. The whip flashed out, here and there, on its merciless errands. John Thornton compressed his lips. Sol-leks was the first to crawl to his feet. Teek followed Joe came next, yelping with pain. Pike made painful efforts. Twice he fell over, when half up, and on the third attempt managed to rise. Buck made no effort. He lay quietly where he had fallen. The lash bit into him again and again, but he neither whined nor struggled. Several times Thornton started, as though to speak, but changed his mind. A moisture came into his eyes, and, as the whipping continued, he arose and walked irresolutely up and down.

This was the first time Buck had failed, in itself sufficient reason to drive Hal into a rage. He exchanged the whip for the customary club. Buck refused to move under the rain of heavy blows which now fell upon him. Like his mates, he was barely able to get up, but, unlike them, he had made up his mind not to get up. He had a vague feeling of impending doom. This had been strong upon him when he pulled

'If you strike that dog again, I'll kill you' he at last
managed to say in a choking voice

in to the bank, and it had not departed from him. What of the thin and rotten ice he had felt under his feet all day, it seemed that he sensed disaster close at hand, out there ahead on the ice where his master was trying to drive him. He refused to stir. So greatly had he suffered, and so far gone was he, that the blows did not hurt much. And as they continued to fall upon him, the spark of life within flickered and went down. It was nearly out. He felt strangely numb. As though from a great distance, he was aware that he was being beaten. The last sensations of pain left him. He no longer felt anything, though very faintly he could hear the impact of the club upon his body. But it was no longer his body, it seemed so far away.

And then, suddenly, without warning, uttering a cry that was inarticulate and more like the cry of an animal, John Thornton sprang upon the man who wielded the club. Hal was hurled backward, as though struck by a falling tree. Mercedes screamed. Charles looked on wistfully, wiping his watery eyes, but did not get up because of his stiffness.

John Thornton stood over Buck, struggling to control himself, too convulsed with rage to speak.

'If you strike that dog again, I'll kill you,' he at last managed to say in a choking voice.

'It's my dog,' Hal replied, wiping the blood from his mouth as he came back. 'Get out of my way, or I'll fix you. I'm going to Dawson.'

Thornton stood between him and Buck, and evinced no intention of getting out of the way. Hal drew his long hunting-knife. Mercedes screamed, cried, laughed and manifested the chaotic abandonment of hysteria. Thornton rapped Hal's knuckles with the axehandle, knocking the knife to the ground. He rapped his knuckles again as he tried to pick it up. Then he stooped, picked it up himself, and with two strokes cut Buck's traces.

Hal had no fight left in him. Besides, his hands were full with his sister, or his arms, rather; while Buck was too near dead to be of further use in hauling the sled. A few minutes later they pulled out from the bank and down the river. Buck heard them go and raised his head to see. Pike was leading, Sol-leks was at the wheel, and between were Joe and Teek. They were limping and staggering. Mercedes was riding the loaded sled. Hal guided at the gee-pole, and Charles stumbled along in the rear.

As Buck watched them, Thornton knelt beside him and with rough, kindly hands searched for broken bones. By the time his search had disclosed nothing more than many bruises and a state of terrible starvation, the sled was a quarter of a mile away. Dog and man watched it crawling along over the ice. Suddenly, they saw its back end drop down, as into a rut, and the gee-pole, with Hal clinging to it, jerk into the air. Mercedes's scream came to their ears. They saw Charles turn and make one step to run back, and then a whole section of ice gave way and dogs and humans disappeared. A yawning hole was all that was to be seen. The bottom had dropped out of the trail.

John Thornton and Buck looked at each other.

'You poor devil,' said John Thornton, and Buck licked his hand.

6   For the Love of a Man

When John Thornton froze his feet in the previous December, his partners had made him comfortable and left him to get well, going on themselves up the river to get out a raft of saw-logs for Dawson. He was still limping slightly at the time he rescued Buck, but with the continued warm weather even the slight limp left him. And here, lying by the river bank through the long spring days, watching the running water, listening lazily to the songs of birds and the hum of nature, Buck slowly won back his strength.

A rest comes very good after one has travelled three thousand miles, and it must be confessed that Buck waxed lazy as his wounds healed, his muscles swelled out, and the flesh came back to cover his bones. For that matter, they were all loafing – Buck, John Thornton, and Skeet and Nig – wating for the raft to come that was to carry them down to Dawson. Skeet was a little Irish setter who early made friends with Buck, who, in a dying condition, was unable to resent her first advances. She had the doctor trait which some dogs possess; and as a mother cat washes her kittens, so she washed and cleansed Buck's wounds. Regularly, each morning, after he had finished his breakfast, she performed her self-appointed task, till he came to look for her ministrations as much as he did for Thornton's. Nig, equally friendly, though less demonstrative, was a huge black dog, half bloodhound and half deerhound, with eyes that laughed and a boundless good nature.

To Buck's surprise these dogs manifested no jealousy toward him. They seemed to share the kindliness and largeness of John

Thornton. As Buck grew stronger they enticed him into all sorts of ridiculous games, in which Thornton himself could not forbear to join; and in this fashion Buck romped through his convalescence and into a new existence. Love, genuine passionate love, was his for the first time. This he had never experienced at Judge Miller's down in the sun-kissed Santa Clara Valley. With the Judge's son, hunting and tramping, it had been a working partnership; with the Judges's grandsons, a sort of pompous guardianship; and with the Judge himself, a stately and dignified friendship. But love that was feverish and burning, that was adoration, that was madness, it had taken John Thornton to arouse.

This man had saved his life, which was something; but, further, he was the ideal master. Other men saw to the welfare of their dogs from a sense of duty and business expediency; he saw to the welfare of his as if they were his own children, because he could not help it. And he saw further. He never forgot a kindly greeting or a cheering word, and to sit down for a long talk with them ('gas' he called it) was as much his delight as theirs. He had a way of taking Buck's head roughly between his hands, and resting his own head upon Buck's, of shaking him back and forth, the while calling him ill names that to Buck were love names. Buck knew no greater joy than that rough embrace and the sound of murmured oaths, and at each jerk back and forth it seemed that his heart would be shaken out of his body so great was its ecstasy. And when, released, he sprang to his feet, his mouth laughing, his eyes eloquent, his throat vibrant with unuttered sounds, and in that fashion remain without movement, John Thornton would reverently exclaim, 'God, you can all but speak!'

Buck had a trick of love expression that was akin to hurt. He would often seize Thornton's hand in his mouth and close so fiercely that the flesh bore impress of his teeth for some time afterward. And as Buck understood the oaths to be love words, so the man understood this feigned bite for a caress.

For the most part, however, Buck's love was expressed in adoration. While he went wild with happiness when Thornton touched him or spoke to him, he did not seek these tokens. Unlike

Skeet, who was wont to shove her nose under Thornton's hand and nudge and nudge till petted, or Nig, who would stalk up and rest his great head on Thornton's knee, Buck was content to adore at a distance. He would lie by the hour, eager, alert, at Thornton's feet looking up into his face, dwelling upon it, studying it, following with keenest interest each fleeting expression, every movement or change of feature. Or, as chance might have it, he would lie farther away, to the side or rear, watching the outlines of the man and the occasional movements of his body. And often, such was the communion in which they lived, the strength of Buck's gaze would draw John Thornton's head around, and he would return the gaze, without speech, his heart shining out of his eyes as Buck's heart shone out.

For a long time after his rescue, Buck did not like Thornton to get out of his sight. From the moment he left the tent to when he entered it again, Buck would follow at his heels. His transient masters since he had come into the Northland had bred in him fear that no master could be permanent. He was afraid that Thorton would pass out of his life as Perrault and François and Scotch half-breed had passed out. Even in the night, in his dreams, he was haunted by this fear. At such times he would shake off sleep and creep through the chill to the flap of the tent, where he would stand and listen to the sound of his master's breathing.

But in spite of this great love he bore John Thornton, which seemed to bespeak the soft civilising influence, the strain of the primitive, which the Northland had aroused in him, remained alive and active. Faithfulness and devotion, things born of fire and roof, were his, yet he retained his wildness and wiliness. He was a thing of the wild, come in from the wild to sit by John Thornton's fire, rather than a dog of the soft Southland stamped with the marks of generations of civilisation. Because of his very great love, he could not steal from this man, but from any man, in any other camp, he did not hesitate an instant; while the cunning with which he stole enabled him to escape detection.

His face and body were scored by the teeth of many dogs, and he fought as fiercely as ever and more shrewdly. Skeet and Nig were too good-natured for quarrelling – besides, they belonged to John Thornton; but the strange dog, no matter what the breed or valour, swiftly acknowledged Buck's supremacy or found himself struggling for life with a terrible antagonist. And Buck was merciless. He had learned well the law of club and fang, and he never forewent an advantage or drew back from a foe he had started on the way to Death. He had lessoned from Spitz, and from the chief fighting dogs of the police and mail, and knew there was no middle course. He must master or be mastered; while to show mercy was a weakness. Mercy did not exist in the primordial life. It was misunderstood for fear, and such misunderstandings made for death. Kill or be killed, eat or be eaten, was the law; and this mandate, down out of the depths of Time, he obeyed.

He was older than the days he had seen and the breaths he had drawn. He linked the past with the present, and the eternity behind him throbbed through him in a mighty rhythm to which he swayed as the tides and season swayed. He sat by John Thornton's fire, a broad-breasted dog, white-fanged and long-furred; but behind him were the shades of all manner of dogs, half-wolves and wild wolves, urgent and prompting, tasting the savour of the meat he ate, thirsting for the water he drank, scenting the wind with him, listening with him and telling him the sounds made by the wild life in the forest, dictating his moods, directing his actions, lying down to sleep with him when he lay down, and dreaming with him and beyond him and becoming themselves the stuff of his dreams.

So peremptorily did these shades beckon him, that each day mankind and the claims of mankind slipped father from him. Deep in the forest a call was sounding, and as often as he heard this call, mysteriously thrilling and luring, he felt compelled to turn his back upon the fire and the beaten earth around it, and to plunge into the forest, and on and on, he knew not where or why; the call sounding imperiously, deep in the forest. But as often as he gained the soft unbroken earth and the green shade, the love for John Thornton drew him back to the fire again.

Thornton alone held him. The rest of mankind was as nothing. Chance travellers might praise or pet him; but he was cold under it all, and from a too demonstrative man he would get up and walk away. When Thornton's partners, Hans and Pete, arrived on the long-expected raft Buck refused to notice them till he learned they were close to Thornton; after that he tolerated them in a passive sort of way, accepting favours from them as though he favoured them by accepting. They were of the same large type as Thornton, living close to the earth, thinking simply and seeing clearly; and ere they swung the raft into the big eddy by the saw-mill at Dawson, they understood Buck and his ways, and did not insist upon an intimacy such as obtained with Skeet and Nig.

For Thornton, however, his love seemed to grow and grow. He, alone among men, could put a pack upon Buck's back in the summer travelling. Nothing was too great for Buck to do, when Thornton commanded. One day (they had grub-staked themselves from the proceeds of the raft and left Dawson for the head-waters of the Tanana) the men and dogs were sitting on the crest of a cliff which fell away, straight down, to naked bed-rock three hundred feet below. John Thornton was sitting near the edge. Buck at his shoulder. A thoughtless whim seized Thornton, and he drew the attention of Hans and Pete to the experiment he had in mind. 'Jump, Buck!' he commanded, sweeping his arm out and over the chasm. The next instant he was grappling with Buck on the extreme edge, while Hans and Pete were dragging them back into safety.

'It's uncanny,' Pete said, after it was over and they had caught their speech.

Thornton shook his head. 'No, it is splendid, and it is terrible, too. Do you know, it sometimes makes me afraid.'

'I'm not hankering to be the man that lays hands on you while he's around,' Pete announced conclusively, nodding his head toward Buck.

'By Jingo!' was Hans' contribution. 'Not mineself either.'

It was at Circle City, ere the year was out, that Pete's apprehensions were realised. 'Black' Burton, a man evil-tempered and malicious, had been picking a quarrel with a tenderfoot at the bar, when Thornton stepped good-naturedly between. Buck, as was his custom, was lying in a corner, head on paws, watching his master's every action. Burton struck out, without warning, straight from the shoulder. Thorton was sent spinning, and saved himself from falling only by clutching the rail of the bar.

Those who were looking on heard what was neither bark nor yelp, but a something which is best described as a roar, and they saw Buck's body rise up in the air as he left the floor for Burton's throat. The man saved his life by instinctively throwing out his arm, but was hurled backward to the floor with Buck on top of him. Buck loosed his teeth from the flesh of the arm and drove in again for the throat. This time the man succeeded only in partly blocking, and his throat was torn open. Then the crowd was upon Buck, and he was driven off; but while a surgeon checked the bleeding, he prowled up and down, growling furiously, attempting to rush in, and being forced back by an array of hostile clubs. A 'miners' meeting', called on the spot, decided that the dog had sufficient provocation, and Buck was discharged. But his reputation was made, and from that day his name spread through every camp in Alaska.

Later on, in the fall of the year, he saved John Thornton's life in quite another fashion. The three partners were lining a long and narrow poling-boat down a bad stretch of rapids on the Forty-Mile Creek. Hans and Pete moved along the bank, snubbing with a thin Manila rope from tree to tree, while Thornton remained in the boat, helping the descent by means of a pole, and shouting directions to the shore. Buck, on the bank worried and anxious, kept abreast of the boat, his eyes never off his master.

At a particularly bad spot where a ledge of barely submerged rocks jutted out into the river, Hans cast off the rope, and, while Thornton poled the boat out into the stream, ran down the bank with the end in his hand to snub the boat when it had cleared the ledge. This it did, and was flying down-stream in a current as swift as a mill-race, when Hans checked it with the rope and checked too suddenly. The boat flirted over and snubbed into the bank bottom up, while Thornton, flung sheer out of it, was carried down-stream toward the worst part of the rapids, a stretch of wild water in which no swimmer could live.

Buck had sprung in on the instant; and at the end of three hundred yards, amid a mad swirl of water, he overhauled Thornton. When he felt him grasp his tail, Buck headed for the bank, swimming with all his splendid strength. But the progress shoreward was slow; the progress down-stream amazingly rapid. From below came the fatal roaring where the wild current went wilder and was rent in shreds and spray by the rocks which thrust through like the teeth of an enormous comb. the suck of the water as it took the beginning of the last steep pitch was frightful, and Thornton knew that the shore was impossible. He scraped furiously over a rock, bruised across a second, and struck a third with crushing force. He clutched its slippery top with both hands, releasing Buck, and above the roar of the churning water shouted: Go, Buck! Go!'

Buck could not hold his own, and swept on down-stream, struggling desperately, but unable to win back. When he heard Thornton's command repeated, he partly reared out of the water, throwing his head high as though for a last look, then turned obediently toward the bank. He swam powerfully and was dragged ashore by Pete and Hans at the very point where swimming ceased to be possible and destruction began.

They knew that the time a man could cling to a slippery rock in the face of that driving current was a matter of minutes, and they ran as fast as they could up the bank to a point far above where Thornton was hanging on. They attached the line with which they had been snubbing the boat to Buck's neck and shoulders, being careful that it should neither strangle him nor impede his swimming and launched him into the stream. He struck out boldly but not straight enough into the stream. He discovered the mistake too late, when Thornton was abreast of him and a bare half-dozen strokes away while he was being carried helplessly past.

Hans promptly snubbed with the rope, as though Buck were a boat. The rope thus tightening on him in the sweep of the current, he was jerked under the surface, and under the surface he remained till his body struck against the bank and he was hauled out. He was half drowned, and Hans and Pete threw themselves upon him, pounding the breath into him and the water out of him. He staggered to his feet and fell down. The faint sound of Thornton's voice came to them, and though they could not make out the words of it, they knew that he was in his extremity. His master's voice acted on Buck like an electric shock. He sprang to his feet and ran up the bank ahead of the men to the point of his previous departure.

Again the rope was attached and he was launched, and again he struck out, but this time straight into the stram. He had miscalculated once, but he would not be guilty of it a second time. Hans paid out the rope, permitting no slack, while Pete kept it clear of coils. Buck held on till he was on a line straight above Thornton; then he turned, and with the speed of an express train headed down upon him. Thornton saw him coming, and, as Buck struck him like a battering ram, with the whole force of the current behind him, he reached up and closed with both arms around the shaggy neck. Hans snubbed the rope around the tree, and Buck and Thornton were jerked under the water. Strangling, suffocating, sometimes one uppermost and sometimes the other, dragging over the jagged bottom, smashing against rocks and snags, they veered in to the bank.

Thornton came to, belly downward and being violently propelled back and forth across a drift log by Hans and Pete. His first glance was for Buck, over whose limp and apparently lifeless body Nig was setting up a howl, while Skeet was licking the wet face and closed eyes. Thornton was himself bruised and battered, and he went carefully over Buck's body, when he had been brought around, finding three broken ribs.

'That settles it,' he announced. 'We camp right here.' And camp they did, till Buck's ribs knitted and he was able to travel.

That winter, at Dawson, Buck performed another exploit, not so heroic, perhaps, but one that put his name many notches higher on the totem-pole of Alaskan fame. This exploit was particularly gratifying to the three men; for they stood in need of the outfit which it furnished, and were enabled to make a long-desired trip into the virgin East, where miners had not yet appeared. It was brought about by a conversation in the Eldorado Saloon, in which men waxed boastful of

their favourite dogs. Buck, because of his record, was the target for
these men, and Thornton was driven stoutly to defend him. At the end
of half an hour one man stated that his dog could start a sled with five
hundred pounds and walk off with it; a second bragged six hundred for
his dog; and a third, seven hundred.

'Pooh! pooh!' said John Thornton; 'Buck can start a thousand
pounds.'

'And break it out? and walk off with it for a hundred yards?'
demanded Matthewson, a Bonanza King, he of the seven hundred
vaunt.

'And break it out, and walk off with it for a hundred yards,' John
Thornton said coolly.

'Well.' Matthewson said, slowly and deliberately, so that all could
hear, 'I've got a thousand dollars that says he can't. And there it is.' So
saying, he slammed a sack of gold dust of the size of a bologna sausage
down upon the bar.

Nobody spoke. Thornton's bluff, if bluff it was, had been called.
He could feel a flush of warm blood creeping up his face. His tongue
had tricked him. He did not know whether Buck could start a thousand
pounds. Half a ton! The enormousness of it appalled him. He had great
faith in Buck's strength and had often thought him capable of starting
such a load; but never, as now, had he faced the possibility of it, the
eyes of a dozen men fixed upon him, silent and waiting. Further, he
had no thousand dollars; nor had Hans or Pete.

'I've got a sled standing outside now, with twenty fifty-pound
sacks of flour on it,' Matthewson went on, with brutal directness, 'so
don't let that hinder you.'

Thornton did not reply. He did know what to say. He glanced
from face to face in the absent way of a man who has lost the power of
thought and is seeking somewhere to find the thing that will start it
going again. The face of Jim O'Brien, a Mastodon King and old-time
comrade, caught his eyes. It was a cue to him, seeming to rouse him to
do what he would never have dreamed of doing.

'Can you lend me a thousand?' he asked, almost in a whisper.

'Sure,' answered O'Brien, thumping down a plethoric sack by the side of Matthewson's. 'Though it's little faith I'm having, John, that the beast can do the trick.'

The Eldorado emptied its occupants into the street to see the test. The tables were deserted, and the dealers and gamekeepers came forth to see the outcome of the wager and to lay odds. Several hundred men, furred and mittened, banked around the sled within easy distance. Matthewson's sled, loaded with a thousand pounds of flour, had been standing for a couple of hours, and in the intense cold (it was sixty below zero) the runners had frozen fast to the hard-packed snow. Men offered odds of two to one that Buck could not budge the sled. A quibble arose concerning the phrase 'break out'. O'Brien contended it was Thornton's privilege to knock the runners loose, leaving Buck to 'break it out' from a dead standstill. Matthewson insisted that the phrase included breaking the runners from the frozen grip of the snow. A majority of the men who had witnessed the making of the bet decided in his favour, whereat the odds went up to three to one against Buck.

There were no takers. Not a man believed him capable of the feat. Thornton had been hurried into the wager, heavy with doubt, and now that he looked at the sled itself, the concrete fact, with the regular team of ten dogs curled up in the snow before it, the more impossible the task appeared. Matthewson waxed jubilant.

'Three to one!' he proclaimed. 'I'll lay you another thousand at that figure, Thornton. What d'ye say?'

Thornton's doubt was strong in his face, but his fighting spirit was aroused – the fighting spirit that soars above odds, fails to recognise the impossible, and is deaf to all save the clamour for battle. He called Hans and Pete to him. Their sacks were slim, and with his own the three partners could rake together only two hundred dollars. In the ebb of their fortunes, this sum was their total capital; yet they laid it unhesitatingly against Matthewson's six hundred.

The team of ten dogs was unhitched, and Buck, with his own harness, was put into the sled. He had caught the contagion of the excitement, and he felt that in some way he must do a great thing for John Thornton. Murmurs of admiration at his splendid condition, without an ounce of superfluous flesh, and the one hundred and fifty pounds that he weighed were so many pounds of grit and virility. His furry coat shone with the sheen of silk. Down the neck and across the shoulders, his mane, in repose as it was, half bristled and seemed to lift with every movement, as though excess of vigour made each particular hair alive and active. The great breast and heavy fore legs were no more than in proportion with the rest of the body, where the muscles showed in tight rolls underneath the skin. Men felt these muscles and proclaimed them hard as iron, and the odds went down to two to one.

'Gad, sir! Gad, sir!' stuttered a member of the latest dynasty, a king of the Skookum Benches. 'I offer you eight hundred for him, sir, before the test, sir; eight hundred just as he stands.'

Thornton shook his head and stepped to Buck's side.

'You must stand off from him,' Matthewson protested. 'Free play and plenty of room.'

The crowd fell silent; only could be heard the voices of the gamblers vainly offering two to one. Everybody acknowledged Buck a magnificent animal, but twenty fifty-pound sacks of flour bulked too large in their eyes for them to loosen their pouch-strings.

Thornton knelt down by Buck's side. He took his head in his two hands and rested cheek on cheek. He did not playfully shake him, as was his wont, or murmur soft love curses; but he whispered in his ear. 'As you love me, Buck. As you love me,' was what he whispered. Buck whined with suppressed eagerness.

The crowd was watching curiously. The affair was growing mysterious. It seemed like a conjuration. As Thornton got to his feet, Buck seized his mittened hand between his jaws, pressing in with his teeth and releasing slowly, half-reluctantly. It was the answer, in terms not of speech, but of love. Thornton stepped well back.

'Now, Buck,' he said.

Buck tightened the traces, then slacked them for a matter of several inches. It was the way he had learned.

'Gee!' Thornton's voice rang out, sharp in tense silence.

Buck swung to the right, ending the movement in a plunge that took up the slack and with a sudden jerk arrested his one hundred and fifty pounds. The load quivered, and from under the runners arose a crisp crackling.

'Haw!' Thornton commanded.

Buck duplicated the manœuvre, this time to the left. The crackling turned into a snapping, the sled pivoting and the runners slipping and grating several inches to the side. The sled was broken out. Men were holding their breaths, intensely unconscious of the fact.

'Now, MUSH!'

Thornton's command cracked out like a pistol-shot. Buck threw himself forward, tighening the traces with a jarring lunge. His whole body was gathered compactly together in the tremendous effort, the muscles writhing and kotting like live things under the silky fur. His great chest was low to the ground, his head forward and down, while his feet were flying like mad, the claws scarring the hard-packed snow in parallel grooves. The sled swayed and trembled, half-started forward. One of his feet slipped, and one man groaned aloud. Then the sled lurched ahead in what appeared a rapid succession of jerks, though it never really came to a dead stop again . . . half an inch . . . an inch . . . two inches . . . The jerks perceptibly diminished; as the sled gained momentum, he caught them up, till it was moving steadily along.

Men gasped and began to breathe again, unaware that for a moment they had ceased to breathe. Thornton was running behind, encouraging Buck with short, cheery words. The distance had been measured off, and as he neared the pile of firewood which marked the end of the hundred yards, a cheer began to grow and grow, which burst into a roar as he passed the firewood and halted at command. Every man was tearing himself loose, even Matthewson. Hats and mittens were flying in the air. Men were shaking hands, it did not matter with whom, and bubbling over in a general incoherent babel.

But Thornton fell on his knees beside Buck. Head was against head, and he was shaking him back and forth. Those who hurried up heard him cursing Buck and he cursed long and fervently, and softly and lovingly.

'Gad, sir! Gad, sir!' spluttered the Skookum Bench king. 'I'll give a thousand for him, sir, a thousand, sir – twelve hundred sir.'

Thornton rose to his feet. His eyes were wet. The tears were streaming frankly down his cheeks. 'Sir,' he said to the Skookum Bench king, 'no, sir. You can go to hell, sir. It's the best I can do for you, sir.'

Buck seized Thornton's hand in his teeth. Thornton shook him back and forth. As though animated by a common impulse, the onlookers drew back to a respectful distance; nor were they again indiscreet enough to interrupt.

7   The Sounding of the Call

When Buck earned sixteen hundred dollars in five minutes for John Thornton, he made it possible for his master to pay off certain debts and to journey with his partners into the East after a fabled lost mine, the history of which was as old as the history of the country. Many men had sought it; few had found it; and more than a few there were who had never returned from the quest.

This lost mine was steeped in tragedy and shrouded in mystery. No one knew of the first man. The oldest tradition stopped before it got back to him. From the beginning there had been an ancient and ramshackle cabin. Dying men had sworn to it, and to the mine the site of which it marked, clinching their testimony with nuggets that were unlike any known grades of gold in the Northland.

But no living man had looted this treasure house and the dead were dead; wherefore John Thornton and Pete and Hans, with Buck and half a dozen other dogs, faced into the East on an unknown trail to achieve where men and dogs as good as themselves had failed. They sledded seventy miles up the Yukon, swung to the left into the Stewart River, passed the Mayo and the McQuestion, and held on until the Stewart itself became a streamlet, threading the upstanding peaks which marked the backbone of the continent.

John Thornton asked little of man or nature. He was unafraid of the wild. With a handful of salt and a rifle he could plunge into the wilderness and fare wherever he pleased and as long as he pleased. Being in no haste, Indian fashion, he hunted his dinner in the course of the day's travel; and if he failed to find it, like the Indian, he kept on travelling, secure in the knowledge that sooner or later he would come to it. So, on this great journey into the East, straight meat was the bill of fare, ammunition and tools principally made up the load on the sled, and the time-card was drawn upon the limitless future.

To Buck it was boundless delight, this hunting, fishing, and indefinite wandering through strange places. For weeks at a time they would hold on steadily, day after day; and for weeks upon end they would camp, here and there, the dogs loafing and the men burning holes through frozen muck and gravel and washing countless pans of dirt by the heat of the fire. Sometimes they went hungry, sometimes they feasted riotously, all according to the abundance of game and the fortune of hunting. Summer arrived, and dogs and men, packed on their backs, rafted across blue mountain lakes, and descended or ascended unknown rivers in slender boats whipsawed from the standing forest.

Two months came and went, and back and forth they twisted through the uncharted vastness, where no men were yet where men had been if the Lost Cabin were true. They went across divides in summer blizzards, shivered under the midnight sun on naked mountains between the timber line and the eternal snows, dropped into summer valleys amid swarming gnats and flies, and in the shadows of glaciers picked strawberries and flowers as ripe and fair as any the Southland could boast. In the fall of the year they penetrated a weird lake country, sad and silent, where wild-fowl had been, but where then there was no life nor sign of life – only the blowing of chill winds, the forming of ice in sheltered places, and the melancholy rippling of waves on lonely beaches.

And through another winter they wandered on the obliterated trails of men who had gone before. Once, they came upon a path blazed through the forest, an ancient path, and the Lost Cabin seemed very near. But the path began nowhere and ended nowhere, and it remained mystery, as the man who made it and the reason he made it remained mystery. Another time they chanced upon the time-graven wreckage of a hunting lodge, and amid the shreds of rotted blankets John Thornton found a long-barrelled flint-lock. He knew it for a Hudson

Bay Company gun of the young days in the Northwest, when such a gun was worth its height in beaver skins packed flat. And that was all — no hint as to the man who in an early day had reared the lodge and left the gun among the blankets.

Spring came on once more, and at the end of all their wandering they found, not the Lost Cabin, but a shallow placer in a broad valley where the gold showed like yellow butter across the bottom of the washing-pan. They sought no farther. Each day they worked earned them thousands of dollars in clean dust and nuggets, and they worked every day. The gold was sacked in moose-hide bags, fifty pounds to the bag, and piled like so much firewood outside the spruce-bough lodge. Like giants they toiled, days flashing on the heels of days like dreams as they heaped the treasure up.

There was nothing for the dogs to do, save the hauling in of meat now and again that Thornton killed, and Buck spent long hours musing by the fire. The vision of the short-legged hairy man came to him more frequently now that there was little work to be done; and often, blinking by the fire, Buck wandered with him in that other world which he remembered.

The salient thing of this other world seemed fear. When he watched the hairy man sleeping by the fire, head between his knees, and hands clasped above, Buck saw that he slept restlessly, with many starts and awakenings, at which times he would peer fearfully into the darkness and fling more wood upon the fire. Did they walk by the beach of a sea, where the hairy man gathered shell-fish and ate them as he gathered, it was with eyes that roved everywhere for hidden danger and with legs prepared to run like the wind at its first appearance. Through the forest they crept noiselessly, Buck at the hairy man's heels; and they were alert and vigilant, the pair of them, ears twitching and moving and nostrils quivering, for the man heard and smelled as keenly as Buck. The hairy man could spring up into the trees and travel ahead as fast as on the ground, swinging by the arms from limb to limb, sometimes a dozen feet apart, letting go and catching, never falling, never missing his grip. In fact, he seemed as much at home among the trees as on the ground; and Buck had memories of nights of vigil spent beneath trees wherein the hairy man roosted, holding on tightly as he slept.

And closely akin to the visions of the hairy man was the call still sounding in the depths of the forest. It filled him with a great unrest and strange desires. It caused him to feel a vague, sweet gladness, and he was aware of wild yearnings and stirrings for he knew not what. Sometimes he pursued the call into the forest, looking for it as though it were a tangible thing, barking soflty or defiantly, as the mood might dictate. He would thrust his nose into the cool wood moss, or into the black soil where long grasses grew, and snort with joy at the fat earth smells; or he would crouch for hours, as if in concealment, behind fungus-covered trunks of fallen trees, wide-eyed and wide-eared to all that moved and sounded about him. It might be, lying thus, that he hoped to surprise this call he could not understand. But he did not know why he did these various things. He was impelled to do them, and did not reason about them at all.

Irresistible impulses seized him. He would be lying in camp, dozing lazily in the heat of the day, when suddenly his head would lift and his ears cock up, intent and listening, and he would spring to his feet and dash away, and on and on, for hours, through the forest aisles and across the open spaces where the niggerheads bunched. He loved to run down dry watercourses, and to creep and spy upon the bird life in the woods. For a day at a time he would lie in the underbrush where he could watch the partridges drumming and strutting up and down. But especially he loved to run in the dim twilight of the summer midnights, listening to the subdued and sleepy murmurs of the forest, reading signs and sounds as man may read a book, and seeking for the mysterious something that called – called, waking or sleeping, at all times, for him to come.

One night he sprang from sleep with a start, eager-eyed, nostrils quivering and scenting, his mane bristling in recurrent waves. From the forest came the call (or one note of it, for the call was many noted), distinct and definite as never before – a long-drawn howl, like, yet unlike, any noise made by husky dog. And he knew it, in the old familiar way, as a sound heard before. He sprang through the sleeping camp and in swift silence dashed through the woods. As he drew closer to the cry he went more slowly, with caution in every movement, till he came to an open place among the trees, and looking out saw, erect on haunches, with nose pointed to the sky, a long, lean timber wolf.

He had made no noise yet it ceased from its howling and tried to sense his presence. Buck stalked into the open, half crouching, body gathered compactly together, tail straight and stiff, feet falling with unwonted care. Every movement advertised commingled threatening and overture of friendliness. It was the menacing truce that marks the meeting of wild beasts that prey. But the wolf fled at sight of him. He followed, with wild leapings, in a frenzy to overtake. He ran him into a blind channel, in the bed of the creek, where a timber jam barred the way. The wolf whirled about, pivoting on his hind legs after the fashion of Joe and of all cornered husky dogs, snarling and bristling, clipping his teeth together in a continuous and rapid succession of snaps.

Buck did not attack, but circled about him and hedged him in with friendly advances. The wolf was suspicious and afraid; for Buck made three of him in weight, while his head barely reached Buck's shoulder. Watching his chance, he darted away, and the chase was resumed. Time and again he was cornered, and the thing repeated, though he was in poor condition, or Buck could not so easily have overtaken him. He would run till Buck's head was even with his flank, when he would whirl around at bay, only to dash away again at the first opportunity.

But in the end Buck's pertinacity was rewarded; for the wolf, finding that no harm was intended, finally sniffed noses with him. Then they became friendly, and played about in the nervous, half-coy way with which fierce beasts belie their fierceness. After some time of this the wolf started off at an easy lope in a manner that plainly showed he was going somewhere. He made it clear to Buck that he was to come, and they ran side by side through the sombre twilight, straight up the creek bed, into the gorge from which it issued, and across the bleak divide where it took its rise.

On the opposite slope of the watershed they came down into a level country where were great stretches of forest and many streams, and through these great stretches they ran steadily, hour after hour, the

Then he sat down, pointed his nose upward and howled

sun rising higher and the day growing warmer. Buck was wildly glad. He knew he was at last answering the call, running by the side of his wood brother toward the place from where the call surely came. Old memories were coming upon him fast, and he was stirring to them as of old he stirred to the realities of which they were the shadows. He had done this thing before, somewhere in that other and dimly re-membered world, and he was doing it again, now, running free in the open, the unpacked earth underfoot, the wide sky overhead.

They stopped by a running stream to drink, and, stopping, Buck remembered John Thornton. He sat down. The wolf started on to-ward the place from where the call surely came, then returned to him, sniffing noses and making actions as though to encourage him. But Buck returned about and started slowly on the back track. For the better part of an hour the wild brother ran by his side, whining softly. Then he sat down, pointed his nose upward, and howled. It was a mournful howl, and as Buck held steadily on his way he heard it grow faint and fainter until it was lost in the distance.

John Thornton was eating dinner when Buck dashed into camp and sprang upon him in a frenzy of affection, overturning him, scrambling upon him, licking his face, biting his hand – 'playing the general tom-fool,' as John Thornton characterised it, the while he shook Buck back and forth and cursed him lovingly.

For two days and nights Buck never left camp, never let Thornton out of his sight. He followed him about at his work, watching him while he ate, saw him into his blankets at night and out of them in the morning. But after two days the call in the forest began to sound more imperiously than ever. Buck's restlessness came back on him, and he was haunted by recollections of the wild brother, and of the smiling land beyond the divide and the run side by side through the wide forest stretches. Once again he took to wandering in the woods, but the wild brother came no more; and though he listened through long vigils, the mournful howl was never raised.

He began the sleep out at night, staying away from the camp for days at a time; and once he crossed the divide at the head of the creek and went down into the land of timber and streams. There he wandered

for a week, seeking vainly for fresh signs of the wild brother, killing his
meat as he travelled and travelling with the long easy lope that seems
never to tire. He fished for salmon in a broad stream that emptied
somewhere into the sea, and by this stream he killed a large black bear,
blinded by the mosquitoes while likewise fishing, and raging through
the forest helpless and terrible. Even so, it was a hard fight, and it
aroused the last latent remnants of Buck's ferocity. And two days later,
when he returned to his kill and found a dozen wolverenes quarrelling
over the spoil, he scattered them like chaff; and those that fled left two
behind who would quarrel no more.

The blood-longing became stronger than ever before. He was a
killer, a thing that preyed, living on the things that lived, unaided,
alone, by virtue of his own strength and prowess, surviving triumphantly in a hostile environment where only the strong survived.
Because of all this he became possessed of a great pride in himself,
which communicated itself like a contagion to his physical being. It
advertised itself in all his movements, was apparent in the play of every
muscle, spoke plainly as speech in the way he carried himself and made
his glorious furry coat if anything more glorious. But for the stray
brown on his muzzle and above his eyes, and for the splash of white
hair that ran midmost down his chest, he might well have been
mistaken for a gigantic wolf, larger that the largest of the breed. From
his St Bernard father he had inherited size and weight, but it was his
shepherd mother who had given shape to that size and weight. His
muzzle was the long wolf muzzle, save that it was larger than the
muzzle of any wolf; and his head, somewhat broader, was the wolf
head on a massive scale.

His cunning was wolf cunning, and wild cunning; his intelligence,
shepherd intelligence and St Bernard intelligence; and all this, plus an
experience gained in the fiercest of schools, made him as formidable a
creature as any that roamed the wild. A carnivorous animal, living on a
straight meat diet, he was in full flower, at the high tide of his life, over-
spilling with vigour and virility. When Thornton passed a caressing
hand along his back, a snapping and cracking followed the hand, each
hair discharging its pent magnetism at the contact. Every part, brain

and body, nerve tissue and fibre, was keyed to the most exquisite pitch; and between all the parts there was a perfect equilibrium or adjustment. To sights and sounds and events which required action, he responded with lightning-like rapidity. Quickly as a husky dog could leap to defend from attack or to attack, he could leap twice as quickly. He saw the movement, or heard sound, and responded in less time than another dog required to compass the mere seeing or hearing. He perceived and determined and responded in the same instant. In point of fact the three actions of perceiving, determining, and responding were sequential; but so infinitesimal were the intervals of time between them that they appeared simultaneous. His muscles were surcharged with vitality, and snapped into play sharply, like steel springs. Life streamed through him in splendid flood, glad and rampant, until it seemed that it would burst him asunder in sheer ecstasy and pour forth generously over the world.

'Never was there such a dog,' said John Thornton one day, as the partners watched Buck marching out of camp.

'When he was made, the mould was broke,' said Pete.

'Py jingo! I t'ink so mineself,' Hans affirmed.

They saw him marching out of camp, but they did not see the instant and terrible transformation which took place as soon as he was within the secrecy of the forest. He no longer marched. At once he became a thing of the wild, stealing along softly, cat-footed, a passing shadow that appeared and disappeared among the shadows. He knew how to take advantage of every cover, to crawl on his belly like a snake, and like a snake to leap and strike. He could take a ptarmigan from its nest, kill a rabbit as it slept, and snap in mid air the little chipmunks fleeing a second too late for the trees. Fish, in open pools, were not too quick for him; nor were beaver, mending their dams, too wary. He killed to eat, not from wantonness; but he preferred to eat what he killed himself. So a lurking humour ran through his deeds, and it was his delight to steal upon the squirrels, and, when he all but had them, to let them go, chattering in mortal fear to the tree-tops.

As the fall of the year came on the moose appeared in greater abundance, moving slowly down to meet the winter in the lower and less rigorous valleys. Buck had already dragged down a stray part-grown calf; but he wished strongly for larger and more formidable quarry, and he came upon it one day on the divide at the head of the creek. A bank of twenty moose had crossed over from the land of streams and timber, and chief among them was a great bull. He was in a savage temper, and, standing over six feet from the ground, was as formidable an antagonist as even Buck could desire. Back and forth the bull tossed his great palmated antlers branching to fourteen points and embracing seven feet within the tips. His small eyes burned with a vicious and bitter light, while he roared with fury at sight of Buck.

From the bull's side, just forward of the flank, protruded a feathered arrow-end, which accounted for his savageness. Guided by that instinct which came from the old hunting days of the primordial world, Buck proceeded to cut the bull out from the herd. It was no slight task. He would bark and dance about in front of the bull, just out of reach of the great antlers and of the terrible splay hoofs which could have stamped his life out with a single blow. Unable to turn his back on the fanged danger and go on, the bull would be driven into paroxysms of rage. At such moments he charged Buck, who retreated craftily, luring him on by a simulated inability to escape. But when he was thus separated from his fellows, two or three of the younger bulls would charge back upon Buck and enable the wounded bull to rejoin the herd.

There is a patience of the wild – dogged, tireless, persistent as life itself – that holds motionless for endless hours the spider in its web, the snake in its coils, the panther in its ambuscade; this patience belongs peculiarly to life when it hunts its living food; and it belonged to Buck as he clung to the flank of the herd, retarding its march, irritating the young bulls, worrying the cows with their half-grown calves, and driving the wounded bull mad with helpless rage. For half a day this continued. Buck multiplied himself, attacking from all sides, envelop-ing the herd in a whirlwind of menace, cutting out his victim as fast as it could rejoin its mates, wearing out the patience of creatures preyed upon, which is a lesser patience than that of creatures preying.

As the day wore along and the sun dropped to its bed in the northwest (the darkness had come back and the fall nights were six hours long), the young bulls retraced their steps more and more reluctantly to the aid of their beset leader. The down-coming winter was harrying them on to the lower levels, and it seemed they could never shake off this tireless creature that held them back. Besides, it was not the life of the herd, or of the young bulls, that was threatened. The life of only one member was demanded, which was a remoter interest than their lives, and in the end they were content to pay the toll.

As twilight fell the old bull stood with lowered head, watching his mates – the cows he had known, the calves he had fathered, the bulls he had mastered – as they shambled on at a rapid pace through the fading light. He could not follow, for before his nose leaped the merciless fanged terror that would not let him go. Three hundredweight more than half a ton he weighed; he had lived a long, strong life, full of fight and struggle, and at the end he faced death at the teeth of a creature whose head did not reach beyond his great knuckled knees.

From then on, night and day, Buck never left his prey, never gave it a moment's rest, never permitted it to browse the leaves of the trees or the shoots of young birch and willow. Nor did he give the wounded bull opportunity to slake his burning thirst in the slender trickling streams they crossed. Often, in desperation, he burst into long stretches of flight. At such times Buck did not attempt to stay him, but loped easily at his heels, satisfied with the way the game was played, lying down when the moose stood still, attacking him fiercely when he strove to eat or drink.

The great head drooped more and more under its tree of horns, and the shambling trot grew weak and weaker. He took to standing for long periods, with nose to the ground and dejected ears dropped limply; and Buck found more time in which to get water for himself and in which to rest. At such moments, panting with red lolling tongue and with eyes fixed upon the big bull, it appeared to Buck that a change was coming over the face of things. He could feel a new stir in the land. As the moose were coming into the land, other kinds of life were coming in. Forest and stream and air seemed palpitant with their presence. The news of it was borne in upon him, not by sight, or sound, or smell, but by some other and subtler sense. He heard nothing, saw nothing, yet knew that the land was somehow different; that through it strange things were afoot and ranging; and he resolved to investigate after he had finished the business in hand.

At last, at the end of the fourth day, he pulled the great moose down. For a day and night he remained by the kill, eating and sleeping, turn and turn about. Then, rested, refreshed and strong, he turned his face toward camp and John Thornton. He broke into the long easy lope, and went on, hour after hour, never at loss for the tangled way, heading straight home through strange country with a certitude of direction that put man and his magnetic needle to shame.

As he held on he became more and more conscious of the new stir in the land. There was life abroad in it different from the life which had had been there throughout the summer. No longer was this fact borne in upon him in some subtle, mysterious way. The birds talked of it, the squirrels chattered about it, the very breeze whispered of it. Several times he stopped and drew in the fresh morning air in great sniffs, reading a message which made him leap on with greater speed. He was oppressed with a sense of calamity happening, if it were no calamity already happened; and as he crossed the last water-shed and dropped down into the valley toward camp, he proceeded with greater caution.

Three miles away he came upon a fresh trail that sent his neck hair rippling and bristling. It led straight toward camp and John Thornton. Buck hurried on, swiftly and stealthily, every nerve straining and tense, alert to the multitudinous details which told a story – all but the end. His nose gave him a varying description of the passage of the life on the heels of which he was travelling. He remarked the pregnant silence of the forest. The bird life had flitted. The squirrels were in hiding. One only he saw – a sleek grey fellow, flattened against a grey dead limb so that he seemed a part of it, a woody excrescence upon the wood itself.

As Buck slid along with the obscureness of a gliding shadow, his nose was jerked suddenly to the side as though a positive force had gripped and pulled it. He followed the new scent into a thicket and found Nig. He was lying on his side, dead where he had dragged himself, an arrow protruding, head and feathers from either side of his body.

A hundred yards farther on, Buck came upon one of the sled-dogs Thornton had bought in Dawson. This dog was thrashing about in a death-struggle, directly on the trail, and Buck passed around him without stopping. From the camp came the faint sound of many voices, rising and falling in a sing-song chant. Bellying forward to the edge of the clearing, he found Hans, lying on his face, feathered with arrows like a porcupine. At the same instant Buck peered out where the spruce-bough lodge had been and saw what made his hair leap straight up on his neck and shoulders. A gust of overpowering rage swept over him. He did not know that he growled, but he growled aloud with a terrible ferocity. For the last time in his life he allowed passion to usurp cunning and reason, and it was because of his great love for John Thornton that he lost his head.

The Yeehats were dancing about the wreckage of the spruce-bough lodge when they heard a fearful roaring and saw rushing upon them an animal the like of which they had never seen before. It was Buck, a live hurricane of fury, hurling himself upon them in a frenzy to destroy. He sprang at the foremost man (it was the chief of the Yeehats), ripping the throat wide open till the rent jugular spouted a fountain of blood. He did not pause to worry the victim, but ripped in passing, with the next bound tearing wide the throat of a second man. There was no withstanding him. He plunged about in their very midst, tearing, rending, destroying, in constant and terrific motion which defied the arrows they discharged at him. In fact, so inconceivably rapid were his movements, and so closely were the Indians tangled together, that they shot one another with the arrows; and one young hunter, hurling a spear at Buck in mid air, drove it through the chest of another hunter with such force that the point broke through the skin of the back and stood out beyond. Then a panic seized the Yeehats, and they fled in terror to the woods, proclaiming as they fled the advent of the Evil Spirit.

And truly Buck was the Fiend incarnate, raging at their heels and dragging them down like deer as they raced through the trees. It was a fateful day for the Yeehats. They scattered far and wide over the country, and it was not till a week later that the last of the survivors gathered together in a lower valley and counted their losses. As for Buck, wearying of the pursuit, he returned to the desolated camp. He found Pete where he had been killed in his blankets in the first moment of surprise. Thornton's desperate struggle was fresh-written on the earth, and Buck scented every detail of it down to the edge of a deep pool. By the edge, head and fore feet in the water, lay Skeet, faithful to the last. The pool itself, muddy and discoloured from the sluice boxes, effectually hid what it contained, and it contained John Thornton; for Buck followed his trace into the water, from which no trace led away.

All day Buck brooded by the pool or roamed restlessly about the camp. Death, as a cessation of movement, as a passing out and away from the lives of the living, he knew, and he knew that John Thornton was dead. It left a great void in him, somewhat akin to hunger, but a void which ached and ached, and which food could not fill. At times when he paused to contemplate the carcasses of the Yeehats, he forgot the pain of it; and at such times he was aware of a great pride in himself – a pride greater than any he had yet experience. He had killed man, the noblest game of all, and he had killed in the face of the law of club and fang. He sniffed the bodies curiously. They had died so easily. It was harder to kill a husky dog than them. They were no match at all, were it not for their arrows and spears and clubs. Thenceforward he would be unafraid of them except when they bore in their hands their arrows, spears, and clubs.

Night came on, and a full moon rose high over the trees into the sky, lighting the land till it lay bathed in ghostly day. And with the coming of the night, brooding and mourning by the pool, Buck became alive to a stirring of the new life in the forest other than that which the Yeehats had made. He stood up, listening and scenting. From far away drifted a faint, sharp yelp, followed by a chorus of similar sharp yelps. As the moments passed the yelps grew closer and louder. Again Buck knew them as things heard in that other world which persisted in his memory. He walked to the centre of the open space and listened. It was the call, the many-noted call, sounding more luringly and compellingly than ever before. And as never before, he was ready to obey. John Thornton was dead. The last tie was broken. Man and the claims of man no longer bound him.

Hunting their living meat, as the Yeehats were hunting it, on the flanks of the migrating moose, the wolf pack had at last crossed over from the land of streams and timber and invaded Buck's valley. Into the clearing where the moonlight streamed, they poured in a silvery flood; and in the centre of the clearing stood Buck, motionless as a statue, waiting their coming. They were awed, so still and large he stood, and a moment's pause fell, till the boldest one leaped straight for him. Like a flash Buck struck, breaking the neck. Then he stood, without movement, as before, the stricken wolf rolling in agony behind him. Three others tried it in sharp succession; and one after the other they drew back, streaming blood from slashed throats or shoulders.

This was sufficient to fling the whole pack forward, pell-mell, crowded together, blocked and confused by its eagerness to pull down the prey. Buck's marvellous quickness and agility stood him in good stead. Pivoting on his hind legs, and snapping and gashing, he was everywhere at once, presenting a front which was apparently unbroken so swiftly did he whirl and guard from side to side. But to prevent them from getting behind him, he was forced back, down past the pool and into the creek bed, till he brought up against a high gravel bank. He worked along to a right angle in the bank which the men had made in the course of mining, and in this angle he came to bay, protected on three sides and with nothing to do but face the front.

And so well did he face it, that at the end of half an hour the wolves drew back discomfited. The tongues of all were out and lolling, the white fangs showing cruelly white in the moonlight. Some were lying down with heads raised and ears pricked forward; others stood on their feet, watching him; and still others were lapping water from the pool. One wolf, long and lean and grey, advanced cautiously, in a friendly manner, and Buck recognised the wild brother with whom he had run for a night and a day. He was whining softly and, as Buck whined, they touched noses.

Then an old wolf, gaunt and battle-scarred, came forward. Buck writhed his lips into the preliminary of a snarl, but sniffed noses with him. Whereupon the old wolf sat down, pointed nose at the moon, and broke out the long wolf howl. The others sat down and howled. And now the call came to Buck in unmistakable accents. He, too, sat down and howled. This over, he came out of his angle and the pack crowded around him, sniffing in half-friendly, half-savage manner. The leaders lifted the yelp of the pack and sprang away into the woods. The wolves swung in behind yelping in chorus. And Buck ran with them, side by side with the wild brother, yelping as he ran.

And here may well end the story of Buck. The years were not many when the Yeehats noted a change in the breed of timber wolves; for some were seen with splashes of brown on head and muzzle, and with a rift of white centring down the chest. But more remarkable than this, the Yeehats tell of a Ghost Dog that runs at the head the pack. They are afraid of this Ghost Dog, for it has cunning greater than they, stealing from their camps in fierce winters, robbing their traps, slaying their dogs, and defying their bravest hunters.

Nay, the tale grows worse. Hunters there are who fail to return to the camp, and hunters there have been whom their tribesmen found with throats slashed cruelly open and with wolf prints about them in the snow greater than the prints of any wolf. Each fall, when the Yeehats follow the movement of the moose, there is a certain valley which they never enter. And women there are who become sad when the word goes over the fire of how the Evil Spirit came to select that valley for an abiding-place.

In the summers there is one visitor, however, to that valley, of which the Yeehats do not know. It is a great, gloriously coated wolf, like, and yet unlike, all other wolves. He crosses alone from the smiling timber land and comes down into an open space among the trees. Here a yellow stream flows from rotted moose-hide sacks and sinks into the ground, with long grasses growing through it and vegetable mould overrunning it and hiding its yellow from the sun; and here he muses for a time, howling once, long and mournfully, ere he departs.

But he is not always alone. When the long winter nights come on and the wolves follow their meat into the lower valleys, he may be seen running at the head of the pack, through the pale moonlight or glimmering borealis, leaping gigantic above his fellows, his great throat a-bellow as he sings a song of the younger world, which is the song of the pack.

The Cruise of the 'Dazzler'

The Cruise
of the
'Dazzler'

Jack London

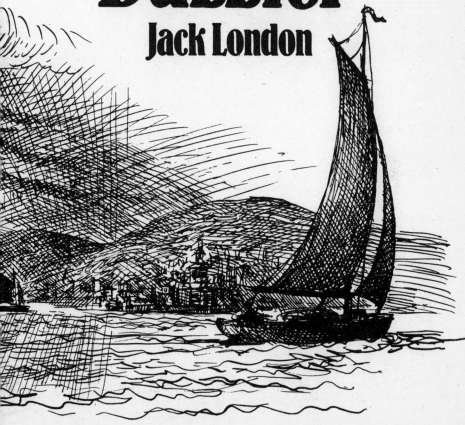

Contents

List of Illustrations

1   Brother and Sister

They ran across the shining sand, the Pacific thundering its long surge
at their backs, and when they gained the roadway leaped upon bicycles
and dived at faster pace into the green avenues of the park. There were
three of them, three boys, in as many bright-coloured sweaters, and
they 'scorched' along the cycle path as dangerously near the speed
limit as is the custom of boys in bright-coloured sweaters to go. They
may have exceeded the speed limit. A mounted park policeman
thought so, but was not sure, and contented himself with cautioning
them as they flashed by. They acknowledged the warning promptly,
and on the next turn of the path as promptly forgot it, which is also a
custom of boys in bright-coloured sweaters.

Shooting out through the entrance to Golden Gate Park, they
turned into San Francisco, and took the long sweep of the descending
hills at a rate that caused pedestrians to turn and watch them
anxiously. Through the city streets the bright sweaters flew, turning
and twisting to escape climbing the steeper hills, and, when the steep
hills were unavoidable, doing stunts to see which would first gain the
top.

The boy who more often hit up the pace, led the scorching, and
instituted the stunts was called Joe by his companions. It was 'follow
the leader,' and he led, the merriest and boldest in the bunch. But as
they pedalled into the Western Addition, among the large and
comfortable residences, his laughter became less loud and frequent,
and he unconsciously lagged in the rear. At Laguna and Vallejo streets
his companions turned off to the right.

'So long, Fred,' he called as he turned his wheel to the left. 'So long, Charley.'

'See you tonight!' they called back.

'No – I can't come,' he answered.

'Aw, come on,' they begged.

'No, I've got to dig. So long!'

As he went on alone, his face grew grave and a vague worry came into his eyes. He began resolutely to whistle, but this dwindled away till it was a thin and very subdued little sound, which ceased altogether as he rode up the driveway to a large two-storeyed house.

'Oh, Joe!'

He hesitated before the door to the library. Bessie was there, he knew, studiously working up her lessons. She must be nearly through with them, too, for she was always done before dinner, and dinner could not be many minutes away. As for his lessons, they were as yet untouched. The thought made him angry. It was bad enough to have one's sister – and two years younger at that – in the same grade, but to have her continually head and shoulders above him in scholarship was a most intolerable thing. Not that he was dull. No one knew better than himself that he was not dull. But somehow – he did not quite know how – his mind was on other things and he was usually unprepared.

'Joe – please come here.' There was the slightest possible plaintive note in her voice this time.

'Well?' he said, thrusting aside the portière with an impetuous movement.

He said it gruffly, but he was half sorry for it the next instant when he saw a slender little girl regarding him with wistful eyes across the big reading table heaped with books. She was curled up, with pencil and pad, in an easy chair of such generous dimensions that it made her seem more delicate and fragile than she really was.

'What is it, Sis?' he asked more gently, crossing over to her side.

She took his hand in hers and pressed it against her cheek, and as he stood beside her came closer to him with a nestling movement.

'What is the matter, Joe dear?' she asked softly. 'Won't you tell me?'

He remained silent. It struck him as ridiculous to confess his troubles to a little sister, even if her reports *were* higher than his. And the little sister struck him as ridiculous to demand his troubles of him. 'What a soft cheek she has!' he thought as she pressed her face gently against his hand. If he could but tear himself away – it was all so foolish! Only he might hurt her feelings, and, in his experience, girls' feelings were very easily hurt.

She opened his fingers and kissed the palm of his hand. It was like a rose leaf falling; it was also her way of asking her question over again.

'Nothing's the matter,' he said decisively. And then, quite inconsistently, he blurted out, 'Father!'

His worry was now in her eyes. 'But father is so good and kind, Joe,' she began. 'Why don't you try to please him? He doesn't ask much of you, and it's all for your own good. It's not as though you were a fool, like some boys. If you would only study a little bit——'

'That's it! Lecturing!' he exploded, tearing his hand roughly away. 'Even you are beginning to lecture me now. I suppose the cook and the stableboy will be at it next.'

He shoved his hands into his pockets and looked forward into a melancholy and desolate future filled with interminable lectures and lecturers innumerable.

'Was that what you wanted me for?' he demanded, turning to go.

She caught at his hand again. 'No, it wasn't; only you looked so worried that I thought – I——' Her voice broke, and she began again freshly. 'What I wanted to tell you was that we're planning a trip across the bay to Oakland, next Saturday, for a tramp in the hills.'

'Who's going?'

'Myrtle Hayes——'

'What! That little softy?' he interrupted.

'I don't think she is a softy,' Bessie answered with spirit. 'She's one of the sweetest girls I know.'

'Which isn't saying much, considering the girls you know. But go on. Who are the others?'

'Pearl Sayther, and her sister Alice, and Jessie Hilborn, and Sadie French, and Edna Crothers. That's all the girls.'

Joe sniffed disdainfully. 'Who are the fellows, then?'

'Maurice and Felix Clement, Dick Schofield, Burt Layton, and——'

'That's enough. Milk-and-water chaps, all of them.'

'I – I wanted to ask you and Fred and Charley,' she said in a quavering voice. 'That's what I called you in for – to ask you to come.'

'And what are you going to do?' he asked.

'Walk, gather wild flowers – the poppies are all out now – eat luncheon at some nice place, and – and——'

'Come home,' he finished for her.

Bessie nodded her head. Joe put his hands in his pockets again, and walked up and down.

'A sissy outfit, that's what it is,' he said abruptly; 'and a sissy programme. None of it for me, please.'

She tightened her trembling lips and struggled on bravely. 'What would you rather do?' she asked.

'I'd sooner take Fred and Charley and go off somewhere and do something – well, anything.'

He paused and looked at her. She was waiting patiently for him to proceed. He was aware of his inability to express in words what he felt and wanted, and all his trouble and general dissatisfaction rose up and gripped hold of him.

'Oh, you can't understand!' he burst out. 'You can't understand. You're a girl. You like to be prim and neat, and to be good in deportment and ahead in your studies. You don't care for danger and adventure and such things, and you don't care for boys who are rough, and have life and go in them, and all that. You like good little boys in white collars, with collars always clean and hair always combed, who like to stay in at recess and be petted by the teacher and told how they're always up in their studies; nice little boys who never get into scrapes – who are too busy walking around and picking flowers and eating lunches with girls, to get into scrapes. Oh, I know the kind – afraid of their own shadows, and no more spunk in them than in so many sheep. That's what they are – sheep. Well, I'm not a sheep, and there's no more to be said. And I don't want to go on your picnic, and, what's more, I'm not going.'

The tears welled up in Bessie's brown eyes, and her lips were trembling. This angered him unreasonably. What were girls good for, anyway? – always blubbering, and interfering, and carrying on. There was no sense in them.

'A fellow can't say anything without making you cry,' he began, trying to appease her. 'Why, I didn't mean anything, Sis. I didn't, sure. I——'

He paused helplessly and looked down at her. She was sobbing, and at the same time shaking with the effort to control her sobs, while big tears were rolling down her cheeks.

'Oh, you – you girls!' he cried, and strode wrathfully out of the room.

2 'The Draconian Reforms'

A few minutes later, and still wrathful, Joe went in to dinner. He ate silently, though his father and mother and Bessie kept up a genial flow of conversation. There she was, he communed savagely with his plate, crying one minute, and the next all smiles and laughter. Now that wasn't his way. If *he* had anything sufficiently important to cry about, rest assured he wouldn't get over it for days. Girls were hypocrites, that was all there was to it. They didn't feel one hundredth part of all that they said when they cried. It stood to reason that they didn't. It must be that they just carried on because they enjoyed it. It made them feel good to make other people miserable, especially boys. That was why they were always interfering.

Thus reflecting sagely, he kept his eyes on his plate and did justice to the fare; for one cannot scorch from the Cliff House to the Western Addition via the park without being guilty of a healthy appetite.

Now and then his father directed a glance at him in a certain mildly anxious way. Joe did not see these glances, but Bessie saw them, every one. Mr Bronson was a middle-aged man, well developed and of heavy build, though not fat. His was a rugged face, square-jawed and stern-featured, though his eyes were kindly and there were lines about the mouth that betokened laughter rather than severity. A close examination was not required to discover the resemblance between him and Joe. The same broad forehead and strong jaw characterised them both, and the eyes, taking into consideration the difference of age, were as like as peas from one pod.

'How are you getting on, Joe?' Mr Bronson asked finally. Dinner was over and they were about to leave the table.

'Oh, I don't know,' Joe answered carelessly, and then added: 'We have examinations tomorrow. I'll know then.'

'Whither bound?' his mother questioned, as he turned to leave the room. She was a slender, willowy woman, whose brown eyes Bessie's were, and likewise her tender ways.

'To my room,' Joe answered. 'To work,' he supplemented.

She rumpled his hair affectionately, and bent and kissed him. Mr Bronson smiled approval at him as he went out, and he hurried up the stairs, resolved to dig hard and pass the examinations of the coming day.

Entering his room, he locked the door and sat down at a desk most comfortably arranged for a boy's study. He ran his eye over his textbooks. The history examination came the first thing in the morning, so he would begin on that. He opened the book where a page was turned down, and began to read:

Shortly after the Draconian reforms, a war broke out between Athens and Megara respecting the island of Salamis, to which both cities laid claim.

That was easy; but what were the Draconian reforms? He must look them up. He felt quite studious as he ran over the back pages, till he chanced to raise his eyes above the top of the book and saw on a chair a baseball mask and a catcher's glove. They shouldn't have lost that game last Saturday, he thought, and they wouldn't have, either, if it hadn't been for Fred. He wished Fred wouldn't fumble so. He could hold a hundred difficult balls in succession, but when a critical point came, he'd let go of even a dewdrop. He'd have to send him out in the field and bring in Jones to first base. Only Jones was so excitable. He could hold any kind of a ball, no matter how critical the play was, but there was no telling what he would do with the ball after he got it.

Joe came to himself with a start. A pretty way of studying history! He buried his head in his book and began:

Shortly after the Draconian reforms——

He read the sentence through three times, and then recollected that he had not looked up the Draconian reforms.

A knock came at the door. He turned the pages over with a noisy flutter, but made no answer.

The knock was repeated, and Bessie's 'Joe, dear' came to his ears.

'What do you want?' he demanded. But before she could answer he hurried on: 'No admittance. I'm busy.'

'I came to see if I could help you,' she pleaded. 'I'm all done, and I thought——'

'Of course you're all done!' he shouted. 'You always are!'

He held his head in both hands to keep his eyes on the Book. But the baseball mask bothered him. The more he attempted to keep his mind on the history the more in his mind's eye he saw the mask resting on the chair and all the games in which it had ever played its part.

This would never do. He deliberately placed the book face downward on the desk and walked over to the chair. With a swift sweep he sent both mask and glove hurtling under the bed, and so violently that he heard the mask rebound from the wall.

Shortly after the Draconian reforms, a war broke out between Athens and Megara——

The mask had rolled back from the wall. He wondered if it had rolled back far enough for him to see it. No, he wouldn't look. What did it matter if it had rolled out? That wasn't history. He wondered——

He peered over the top of the book, and there was the mask peeping out at him from under the edge of the bed. This was not to be borne. There was no use attempting to study while that mask was around. He went over and fished it out, crossed the room to the closet, and tossed it inside, then locked the door. That was settled, thank goodness! Now he could do some work.

He sat down again.

Shortly after the Draconian reforms, a war broke out between Athens and Megara respecting the island of Salamis, to which both cities laid claim.

Which was all very well, if he had only found out what the Draconian reforms were. A soft glow pervaded the room, and he suddenly became aware of it. What could cause it? He looked out of the window. The setting sun was slanting its long rays against low-hanging masses of summer clouds, turning them to warm scarlet and rosy red; and it was from them that the red light, mellow and glowing, was flung earthward.

His gaze dropped from the clouds to the bay beneath. The sea breeze was dying down with the day, and off Fort Point a fishing boat was creeping into port before the last light breeze. A little beyond, a tug was sending up a twisted pillar of smoke as it towed a three-masted schooner to sea. His eyes wandered over toward the Marin County shore. The line where land and water met was already in darkness, and long shadows were creeping up the hills toward Mount Tamalpais, which was sharply silhouetted against the western sky.

Oh, if he, Joe Bronson, were only on that fishing boat and sailing in with a deep-sea catch! Or if he were on that schooner, heading out into the sunset, into the world! That was life, that was living, doing something and being something in the world. And, instead, here he was, pent up in a close room, racking his brains about people dead and gone thousands of years before he was born. He jerked himself away from the window as though held there by some physical force, and resolutely carried his chair and history into the farthest corner of the room, where he sat down with his back to the window.

An instant later, so it seemed to him, he found himself again staring out of the window and dreaming. How he had got there he did not know. His last recollection was the finding of a subheading in a page on the righthand side of the book which read: 'The Laws and Constitution of Draco.' And then, evidently like walking in one's sleep, he had come to the window. How long had he been there? he wondered. The fishing boat which he had seen off Fort Point was now crawling into Meiggs's Wharf. This denoted nearly an hour's lapse of time. The sun had long since set; a solemn greyness was brooding over the water, and the first faint stars were beginning to twinkle over the crest of Mount Tamalpais.

He turned, with a sigh, to go back into his corner, when a long whistle, shrill and piercing, came to his ears. That was Fred. He sighed again. The whistle repeated itself. Then another whistle joined it. They were waiting on the corner – lucky fellows!

Well, they wouldn't see him this night. Both whistles arose in duet. He writhed in his chair and groaned. No, they wouldn't see him this night, he reiterated, at the same time rising to his feet. It was certainly impossible for him to join them when he had not yet learned about the Draconian reforms. The same force which had held him to the window now seemed drawing him across the room to the desk. It made him put the history on top of his schoolbooks, and he had the door unlocked and was halfway into the hall before he realised it. He started to return, but the thought came to him that he could go out for a little while and then come back and do his work.

A very little while, he promised himself, as he went downstairs. He went down faster and faster, till at the bottom he was going three steps at a time. He popped his cap on his head and went out of the side entrance in a rush; and ere he reached the corner the reforms of Draco were as far away in the past as Draco himself, while the examinations on the morrow were equally far away in the future.

3 'Brick,' 'Sorrel-Top' and 'Reddy'

'What's up?' Joe asked, as he joined Fred and Charley.

'Kites,' Charley answered. 'Come on. We're tired out waiting for you.'

The three set off down the street to the brow of the hill, where they looked down upon Union Street, far below and almost under their feet. This they called the Pit, and it was well named. Themselves they called the Hill-dwellers, and a descent into the Pit by the Hill-dwellers was looked upon by them as a great adventure.

Scientific kiteflying was one of the keenest pleasures of these three particular Hill-dwellers, and six or eight kites strung out on a mile of twine and soaring into the clouds was an ordinary achievement for them. They were compelled to replenish their kite supply often; for whenever an accident occurred, and the string broke, or a ducking kite dragged down the rest, or the wind suddenly died out, their kites fell into the Pit, from which place they were unrecoverable. The reason for this was the young people of the Pit were a piratical and robber race with peculiar ideas of ownership and property rights.

On a day following an accident to a kite of one of the Hill-dwellers, the selfsame kite could be seen riding the air attached to a string which led down into the Pit to the lairs of the Pit People. So it came about that the Pit People, who were a poor folk and unable to afford scientific kiteflying, developed great proficiency in the art when their neighbours the Hill-dwellers took it up.

There was also an old sailorman who profited by this recreation of the Hill-dwellers; for he was learned in sails and air currents, and being deft of hand and cunning, he fashioned the best-flying kites that could be obtained. He lived in a rattletrap shanty close to the water, where he could still watch with dim eyes the ebb and flow of the tide, and the ships pass out and in, and where he could revive old memories of the days when he, too, went down to the sea in ships.

To reach his shanty from the Hill one had to pass through the Pit, and thither the three boys were bound. They had often gone for kites in the daytime, but this was their first trip after dark, and they felt it to be, as it indeed was, a hazardous adventure.

In simple words, the Pit was merely the cramped and narrow quarters of the poor, where many nationalities crowded together in cosmopolitan confusion, and lived as best they could, amid much dirt and squalor. It was still early evening when the boys passed through on their way to the sailorman's shanty, and no mishap befell them, though some of the Pit boys stared at them savagely and hurled a taunting remark after them, now and then.

The sailorman made kites which were not only splendid fliers but which folded up and were very convenient to carry. Each of the boys bought a few, and, with them wrapped in compact bundles and under their arms, started back on the return journey.

'Keep a sharp lookout for the b'ys,' the kitemaker cautioned them. 'They're like to be cruisin' round after dark.'

'We're not afraid,' Charley assured him; 'and we know how to take care of ourselves.'

Used to the broad and quiet streets of the Hill, the boys were shocked and stunned by the life that teemed in the close-packed quarter. It seemed some thick and monstrous growth of vegetation, and that they were wading through it. They shrank closely together in the tangle of narrow streets as though for protection, conscious of the strangeness of it all, and how unrelated they were to it.

Children and babies sprawled on the sidewalk and under their feet. Bareheaded and unkempt women gossiped in the doorways or passed back and forth with scant marketings in their arms. There was a general odour of decaying fruit and fish, a smell of staleness and putridity. Big hulking men slouched by, and ragged little girls walked gingerly through the confusion with foaming buckets of beer in their hands. There was a clatter and garble of foreign tongues and brogues, shrill cries, quarrels and wrangles, and the Pit pulsed with a great and steady murmur, like the hum of the human hive that it was.

'Phew! I'll be glad when we're out of it,' Fred said.

He spoke in a whisper, and Joe and Charley nodded grimly that they agreed with him. They were not inclined to speech, and they walked as rapidly as the crowd permitted, with much the same feelings as those of travellers in a dangerous and hostile jungle.

And danger and hostility stalked in the Pit. The inhabitants seemed to resent the presence of these strangers from the Hill. Dirty little urchins abused them as they passed, snarling with assumed bravery, and prepared to run away at the first sign of attack. And still other little urchins formed a noisy parade at the heels of the boys, and grew bolder with increasing numbers.

'Don't mind them,' Joe cautioned. 'Take no notice, but keep right on. We'll soon be out of it.'

'No, we're in for it,' said Fred, in an undertone. 'Look there!'

On the corner they were approaching, four or five boys of about their own age were standing. The light from a street lamp fell upon them and disclosed one with vivid red hair. It could be no other than 'Brick' Simpson, the redoubtable leader of a redoubtable gang. Twice within their memory he had led his gang up the Hill and spread panic and terror among the Hill-dwelling young folk, who fled wildly to their homes, while their fathers and mothers hurriedly telephoned for the police.

At sight of the group on the corner, the rabble at the heels of the three boys melted away on the instant with like manifestations of fear. This but increased the anxiety of the boys, though they held boldly on their way.

The red-haired boy detached himself from the group, and stepped before them, blocking their path. They essayed to go around him, but he stretched out his arm.

'Wot yer doin' here?' he snarled. 'Why don't yer stay where yer b'long?'

'We're just going home,' Fred said mildly.

Brick looked at Joe. 'Wot yer got under yer arm?' he demanded.

Joe contained himself and took no heed of him. 'Come on,' he said to Fred and Charley, at the same time starting to brush past the gang leader.

But with a quick blow Brick Simpson struck him in the face, and with equal quickness snatched the bundle of kites from under his arm.

Joe uttered an inarticulate cry of rage, and, all caution flung to the winds, sprang at his assailant.

This was evidently a surprise to the gang leader, who expected least of all to be attacked in his own territory. He retreated backward, still clutching the kites, and divided between desire to fight and desire to retain his capture.

The latter desire dominated him, and he turned and fled swiftly down the narrow side street into a labyrinth of streets and alleys. Joe knew that he was plunging into the wilderness of the enemy's country, but his sense of both property and pride had been offended, and he took up the pursuit hotfooted.

Fred and Charley followed after, though he outdistanced them, and behind came the three other members of the gang, emitting a whistling call while they ran which was evidently intended for the assembling of the rest of the band. As the chase proceeded, these whistles were answered from many different directions, and soon a score of dark figures were tagging at the heels of Fred and Charley, who, in turn, were straining every muscle to keep the swifter-footed Joe in sight.

Brick Simpson darted into a vacant lot, aiming for a 'slip,' as such things are called which are prearranged passages through fences and over sheds and houses and around dark holes and corners, where the unfamiliar pursuer must go more carefully and where the chances are many that he will soon lose the track.

But Joe caught Brick before he could attain his end, and together they rolled over and over in the dirt, locked in each other's arms. By the time Fred and Charley and the gang had come up, they were on their feet, facing each other. 'Wot d' ye want, eh?' the redheaded

With a quick blow Brick Simpson struck him in the face

gangleader was saying in a bullying tone. 'Wot d' ye want? That's wot I wanter know.'

'I want my kites,' Joe answered.

Brick Simpson's eyes sparkled at the intelligence. Kites were something he stood in need of himself.

'Then you've got to fight fer 'em,' he announced.

'Why should I fight for them?' Joe demanded indignantly. 'They're mine.' Which went to show how ignorant he was of the ideas of ownership and property rights which obtained among the People of the Pit.

A chorus of jeers and catcalls went up from the gang, which clustered behind its leader like a pack of wolves.

'Why should I fight for them?' Joe reiterated.

' 'Cos I say so,' Simpson replied. 'An' wot I say goes. Understand?'

But Joe did not understand. He refused to understand that Brick Simpson's word was law in San Francisco, or any part of San Francisco. His love of honesty and right dealing was offended, and all his fighting blood was up.

'You give those kites to me, right here and now,' he threatened, reaching out his hand for them.

But Simpson jerked them away. 'D' ye know who I am?' he demanded. 'I'm Brick Simpson, an' I don't 'low no one to talk to me in that tone of voice.'

'Better leave him alone,' Charley whispered in Joe's ear. 'What are a few kites? Leave him alone and let's get out of this.'

'They're my kites,' Joe said slowly in a dogged manner. 'They're my kites, and I'm going to have them.'

'You can't fight the crowd,' Fred interfered; 'and if you do get the best of him they'll all pile on you.'

The gang, observing this whispered colloquy, and mistaking it for hesitancy on the part of Joe, set up its wolflike howling again.

'Afraid! afraid!' the young roughs jeered and taunted. 'He's too high-toned, he is! Mebbe he'll spoil his nice clean shirt, and then what'll mama say?'

'Shut up!' their leader snapped authoritatively, and the noise obediently died away.

'Will you give me those kites?' Joe demanded, advancing determinedly.

'Will you fight for 'em?' was Simpson's counterdemand.

'Yes,' Joe answered.

'Fight! fight!' the gang began to howl again.

'And it's me that'll see fair play,' said a man's heavy voice.

All eyes were instantly turned upon the man who had approached unseen and made this announcement. By the electric light, shining brightly on them from the corner, they made him out to be a big, muscular fellow, clad in a working-man's garments. His feet were encased in heavy brogans, a narrow strap of black leather held his overalls about his waist, and a black and greasy cap was on his head. His face was grimed with coal dust, and a coarse blue shirt, open at the neck, revealed a wide throat and massive chest.

'An' who're you?' Simpson snarled, angry at the interruption.

'None of yer business,' the newcomer retorted tartly. 'But, if it'll do you any good, I'm a fireman on the China steamers, and, as I said, I'm goin' to see fair play. That's my business. Your business is to give fair play. So pitch in, and don't be all night about it.'

The three boys were as pleased by the appearance of the fireman as Simpson and his followers were displeased. They conferred together for several minutes when Simpson deposited the bundle of kites in the arms of one of his gang and stepped forward.

'Come on, then,' he said, at the same time pulling off his coat.

Joe handed his to Fred, and sprang toward Brick. They put up their fists and faced each other. Almost instantly Simpson drove in a fierce blow and ducked cleverly away and out of reach of the blow which Joe returned. Joe felt a sudden respect for the abilities of his antagonist, but the only effect upon him was to arouse all the doggedness of his nature and make him utterly determined to win.

Awed by the presence of the fireman, Simpson's followers confined themselves to cheering Brick and jeering Joe. The two boys circled round and round, attacking, feinting, and guarding, and now one and then the other getting in a telling blow. Their positions were in marked contrast. Joe stood erect, planted solidly on his feet, with legs wide apart and head up. On the other hand, Simpson crouched till his head was nearly lost between his shoulders, and all the while he was in constant motion, leaping and springing and manœuvring in the execution of a score or more of tricks quite new and strange to Joe.

At the end of a quarter of an hour, both were very tired, though Joe was much fresher. Tobacco, ill food, and unhealthy living were telling on the gang leader, who was panting and sobbing for breath. Though at first (and because of superior skill) he had severely punished Joe, he was now weak and his blows were without force. Growing desperate, he adopted what might be called not an unfair but a mean method of attack: he would manœuvre, leap in and strike swiftly, and then, ducking forward, fall to the ground at Joe's feet. Joe could not strike him while he was down, and so would step back until he could get on his feet again, when the thing would be repeated.

But Joe grew tired of this, and prepared for him. Timing his blow with Simpson's attack, he delivered it just as Simpson was ducking forward to fall. Simpson fell, but he fell over on one side, whither he had been driven by the impact of Joe's fist upon his head. He rolled over and got halfway to his feet, where he remained, crying and gasping. His followers called upon him to get up, and he tried once or twice, but was too exhausted and stunned.

'I give in,' he said. 'I'm licked.'

The gang had become silent and depressed at its leader's defeat. Joe stepped forward.

'I'll trouble you for those kites,' he said to the boy who was holding them.

'Oh, I dunno,' said another member of the gang, shoving in between Joe and his property. His hair was also a vivid red. 'You've got to lick me before you kin have 'em.'

'I don't see that,' Joe said bluntly. 'I've fought and I've won, and there's nothing more to it.'

'Oh, yes, there is,' said the other. 'I'm "Sorrel-top" Simpson. Brick's my brother. See?'

And so, in this fashion, Joe learned another custom of the Pit

People of which he had been ignorant.

'All right,' he said, his fighting blood more fully aroused than ever by the unjustness of the proceeding. 'Come on.'

Sorrel-top Simpson, a year younger than his brother, proved to be a most unfair fighter, and the good-natured fireman was compelled to interfere several times before the second of the Simpson clan lay on the ground and acknowledged defeat.

This time Joe reached for his kites without the slightest doubt that he was to get them. But still another lad stepped in between him and his property. The telltale hair, vividly red, sprouted likewise on this lad's head, and Joe knew him at once for what he was, another member of the Simpson clan. He was a younger edition of his brothers, somewhat less heavily built, with a face covered with a vast quantity of freckles, which showed plainly under the electric light.

'You don't git them there kites till you git me,' he challenged in a piping little voice. 'I'm "Reddy" Simpson, an' you ain't licked the fambly till you've licked me.'

The gang cheered admiringly, and Reddy stripped a tattered jacket preparatory for the fray.

'Git ready,' he said to Joe.

Joe's knuckles were torn, his nose was bleeding, his lip was cut and swollen, while his shirt had been ripped down from throat to waist. Further, he was tired, and breathing hard.

'How many more are there of you Simpsons?' he asked. 'I've got to get home, and if your family's much larger this thing is liable to keep on all night.'

'I'm the last an' the best,' Reddy replied. 'You gits me an' you gits the kites. Sure.'

'All right,' Joe sighed. 'Come on.'

While the youngest of the clan lacked the strength and skill of his elders, he made up for it by a wildcat manner of fighting that taxed Joe severely. Time and again it seemed to him that he must give in to the little whirlwind; but each time he pulled himself together and went doggedly on. For he felt that he was fighting for principle, as his forefathers had fought for principle; also, it seemed to him that the honour of the Hill was at stake, and that he, as its representative, could do nothing less than his very best.

So he held on and managed to endure his opponent's swift and continuous rushes till that young and less experienced person at last wore himself out with his own exertions, and from the ground confessed that, for the first time in its history, the 'Simpson fambly was beat.'

4 The Biter Bitten

But life in the pit at best was a precarious affair, as the three Hill-dwellers were quickly to learn. Before Joe could even possess himself of his kites, his astonished eyes were greeted with the spectacle of all his enemies, the fireman included, taking to their heels in wild flight. As the little girls and urchins had melted away before the Simpson gang, so was melting away the Simpson gang before some new and correspondingly awe-inspiring group of predatory creatures.

Joe heard terrified cries of 'Fish gang!' 'Fish gang!' from those who fled, and he would have fled himself from this new danger, only he was breathless from his last encounter, and knew the impossibility of escaping whatever threatened. Fred and Charley felt mighty longings to run away from a danger great enough to frighten the redoubtable Simpson gang and the valorous fireman, but they could not desert their comrade.

Dark forms broke into the vacant lot, some surrounding the boys and others dashing after the fugitives. That the laggards were overtaken was evidenced by the cries of distress that went up, and when later the pursuers returned, they brought with them the luckless and snarling Brick, still clinging fast to the bundle of kites.

Joe looked curiously at this latest band of marauders. They were young men of from seventeen and eighteen to twenty-three and -four years of age, and bore the unmistakable stamp of the hoodlum class. There were vicious faces among them – faces so vicious as to make Joe's flesh creep as he looked at them. A couple grasped him tightly by the arms, and Fred and Charley were similarly held captive.

'Look here, you,' said one who spoke with the authority of leader, 'we've got to inquire into this. Wot's be'n goin' on here? Wot're you up to, Redhead? Wot you be'n doin'?'

'Ain't be'n doin' nothin',' Simpson whined.

'Looks like it.' The leader turned up Brick's face to the electric light. 'Who's been paintin' you up like that?' he demanded.

Brick pointed at Joe, who was forthwith dragged to the front.

'Wot was you scrappin' about?'

'Kites – my kites,' Joe spoke up boldly. 'That fellow tried to take them away from me. He's got them under his arm now.'

'Oh, he has, has he? Look here, you Brick, we don't put up with stealin' in this territory. See? You never rightly owned nothin'. Come, fork over the kites. Last call.'

The leader tightened his grasp threateningly, and Simpson, weeping tears of rage, surrendered the plunder.

'Wot yer got under yer arm?' the leader demanded abruptly of Fred, at the same time jerking out the bundle. 'More kites, eh? Reg'lar kite factory gone and got itself lost,' he remarked finally, when he had appropriated Charley's bundle. 'Now, wot I wants to know is wot we're goin' to do to you t'ree chaps?' he continued in a judicial tone.

'What for?' Joe demanded hotly. 'For being robbed of our kites?'

'Not at all, not at all,' the leader responded politely; 'but for luggin' kites round these quarters an' causin' all this unseemly disturbance. It's disgraceful; that's wot it is – disgraceful.'

At this juncture, when the Hill-dwellers were the centre of attraction, Brick suddenly wormed out of his jacket, squirmed away from his captors, and dashed across the lot to the slip for which he had been originally headed when overtaken by Joe. Two or three of the gang shot over the fence after him in noisy pursuit. There was much barking and howling of back-yard dogs and clattering of shoes over sheds and boxes. Then there came a splashing of water, as though a barrel of it had been precipitated to the ground. Several minutes later the pursuers returned, very sheepish and very wet from the deluge presented them by the wily Brick, whose voice, high up in the air from some friendly housetop, could be heard defiantly jeering them.

This event apparently disconcerted the leader of the gang, and just as he turned to Joe and Fred and Charley, a long and peculiar whistle came to their ears from the street – the warning signal, evidently, of a scout posted to keep a lookout. The next moment the scout himself came flying back to the main body, which was already beginning to retreat.

'Cops!' he panted.

Joe looked, and he saw two helmeted policemen approaching, with bright stars shining on their breasts.

'Let's get out of this,' he whispered to Fred and Charley.

The gang had already taken to flight, and they blocked the boys' retreat in one quarter, and in another they saw the policemen advancing. So they took to their heels in the direction of Brick Simpson's slip, the policemen hot after them and yelling bravely for them to halt.

But young feet are nimble, and young feet when frightened become something more than nimble, and the boys were first over the fence and plunging wildly through a maze of back yards. They soon found that the policemen were discreet. Evidently they had had experiences in slips, and they were satisfied to give over the chase at the first fence.

No street lamps shed their light here, and the boys blundered along through the blackness with their hearts in their mouths. In one yard, filled with mountains of crates and fruit boxes, they were lost for a quarter of an hour. Feel and quest about as they would, they encountered nothing but endless heaps of boxes. From this wilderness they finally emerged by way of a shed roof, only to fall into another yard, cumbered with countless empty chicken coops.

Farther on they came upon the contrivance which had soaked Brick Simpson's pursuers with water. It was a cunning arrangement. Where the slip led through a fence with a board missing, a long slat was so arranged that the ignorant wayfarer could not fail to strike against it. This slat was the spring of the trap. A light touch upon it was sufficient to disconnect a heavy stone from a barrel perched overhead and nicely balanced. The disconnecting of the stone permitted the barrel to turn over and spill its contents on the one beneath who touched the slat.

The boys examined the arrangement with keen appreciation. Luckily for them, the barrel was overturned, or they too would have received a ducking, for Joe, who was in advance, had blundered against the slat.

'I wonder if this is Simpson's back yard?' he queried softly.

'It must be,' Fred concluded, 'or else the back yard of some member of his gang.'

Charley put his hands warningly on both their arms.

'Hist! What's that?' he whispered.

They crouched down on the ground. Not far away was the sound of someone moving about. Then they heard a noise of falling water, as from a faucet into a bucket. This was followed by steps boldly approaching. They crouched lower, breathless with apprehension.

A dark form passed by within arm's reach and mounted on a box to the fence. It was Brick himself, resetting the trap. They heard him arrange the slat and stone, then right the barrel and empty into it a couple of buckets of water. As he came down from the box to go after more water, Joe sprang upon him, tripped him up, and held him to the ground.

'Don't make any noise,' he said. 'I want you to listen to me.'

'Oh, it's you, is it?' Simpson replied, with such obvious relief in his voice as to make them feel relieved also. 'Wot d' ye want here?'

'We want to get out of here,' Joe said, 'and the shortest way's the best. There's three of us, and you're only one——'

'That's all right, that's all right,' the gang leader interrupted. 'I'd just as soon show you the way out as not. I ain't got nothin' 'gainst you. Come on an' follow me, an' don't step to the side, an' I'll have you out in no time.'

Several minutes later they dropped from the top of a high fence into a dark alley.

'Follow this to the street,' Simpson directed; 'turn to the right two blocks, turn to the right again for three, an' yer on Union. Tra-la-loo.'

They said goodbye, and as they started down the alley received the following advice:

'Nex' time you bring kites along, you'd best leave 'em to home.'

5   Home Again

Following Brick Simpson's directions, they came into Union Street, and without further mishap gained the Hill. From the brow they looked down into the Pit, whence arose that steady, indefinable hum which comes from crowded human places.

'I'll never go down there again, not as long as I live,' Fred said with a great deal of savagery in his voice. 'I wonder what became of the fireman.'

'We're lucky to get back with whole skins,' Joe cheered them philosophically.

'I guess we left our share, and you more than yours,' laughed Charley.

'Yes,' Joe answered. 'And I've got more trouble to face when I get home. Good night, fellows.'

As he expected, the door on the side porch was locked, and he went around to the dining room and entered like a burglar through a window. As he crossed the wide hall, walking softly toward the stairs, his father came out of the library. The surprise was mutual, and each halted aghast.

Joe felt a hysterical desire to laugh, for he thought that he knew precisely how he looked. In reality he looked far worse than he imagined. What Mr Bronson saw was a boy with hat and coat covered with dirt, his whole face smeared with the stains of conflict, and, in particular, a badly swollen nose, a bruised eyebrow, a cut and swollen lip, a scratched cheek, knuckles still bleeding, and a shirt torn open from throat to waist.

'What does this mean, sir?' Mr Bronson finally managed to articulate.

Joe stood speechless. How could he tell, in one brief sentence, all the whole night's happenings? – for all that must be included in his explanation of what his luckless disarray meant.

'Have you lost your tongue?' Mr Bronson demanded with an appearance of impatience.

'I've – I've——'

'Yes, yes,' his father encouraged.

'I've – well, I've been down in the Pit,' Joe succeeded in blurting out.

'I must confess that you look like it – very much like it indeed.' Mr Bronson spoke severely, but if ever by great effort he conquered a smile, that was the time. 'I presume,' he went on, 'that you do not refer to the abiding place of sinners, but rather to some definite locality in San Francisco. Am I right?'

Joe swept his arm in a descending gesture toward Union Street, and said: 'Down there, sir.'

'And who gave it that name?'

'I did,' Joe answered, as though confessing to a specified crime.

'It's most appropriate, I'm sure, and denotes imagination. It couldn't really be bettered. You must do well at school, sir, with your English.'

This did not increase Joe's happiness, for English was the only study of which he did not have to feel ashamed.

And, while he stood thus a silent picture of misery and disgrace, Mr Bronson looked upon him through the eyes of his own boyhood with an understanding which Joe could not have believed possible.

'However, what you need just now is not a discourse, but a bath and court plaster and witch hazel and cold water bandages,' Mr Bronson said, 'so to bed with you. You'll need all the sleep you can get, and you'll feel stiff and sore tomorrow morning, I promise you.'

The clock struck one as Joe pulled the bedclothes around him; and the next he knew he was being worried by a soft, insistent rapping, which seemed to continue through several centuries, until at last, unable to endure it longer, he opened his eyes and sat up.

The day was streaming in through the window – bright and sunshiny day. He stretched his arms to yawn; but a shooting pain darted through all the muscles, and his arms came down more rapidly than they had gone up. He looked at them with a bewildered stare, till suddenly the events of the night rushed in upon him, and he groaned.

The rapping still persisted, and he cried: 'Yes, I hear. What time is it?'

'Eight o'clock,' Bessie's voice came to him through the door. 'Eight o'clock, and you'll have to hurry if you don't want to be late for school.'

'Goodness!' He sprang out of bed precipitately, groaned with the pain from all his stiff muscles, and collapsed slowly and carefully on a chair. 'Why didn't you call me sooner?' he growled.

'Father said to let you sleep.'

Joe groaned again, in another fashion. Then his history book caught his eye, and he groaned yet again and in still another fashion.

'All right,' he called. 'Go on. I'll be down in a jiffy.'

He did come down in fairly brief order; but if Bessie had watched him descend the stairs she would have been astounded at the remarkable caution he observed and at the twinges of pain that every now and then contorted his face. As it was, when she came upon him in the dining room she uttered a frightened cry and ran over to him.

'What's the matter, Joe?' she asked tremulously. 'What has happened?'

'Nothing,' he grunted, putting sugar on his porridge.

'But surely——' she began.

'Please don't bother me,' he interrupted. 'I'm late, and I want to eat my breakfast.'

And just then Mrs Bronson caught Bessie's eye, and that young lady, still mystified, made haste to withdraw herself.

Joe was thankful to his mother for that, and thankful that she refrained from remarking upon his appearance. Father had told her; that was one thing sure. He could trust her not to worry him; it was never her way.

And, meditating in his way, he hurried through with his solitary breakfast, vaguely conscious in an uncomfortable way that his mother was fluttering anxiously about him. Tender as she always was, he noticed that she kissed him with unusual tenderness as he started out with his books swinging at the end of a strap; and he also noticed, as he turned the corner, that she was still looking after him through the window.

But of more vital importance than that, to him, was his stiffness and soreness. As he walked along, each step was an effort and a torment. Severely as the reflected sunlight from the cement sidewalk hurt his bruised eye, and severely as his various wounds pained him, still more severely did he suffer from his muscles and joints. He had never imagined such stiffness. Each individual muscle in his whole body protested when called upon to move. His fingers were badly swollen, and it was agony to clasp and unclasp them; while his arms were sore from wrist to elbow. This, he said to himself, was caused by the many blows which he had warded off from his face and body. He wondered if Brick Simpson was in similar plight, and the thought of their mutual misery made him feel a certain kinship for that redoubtable young ruffian.

When he entered the school yard he quickly became aware that he was the centre of attraction for all eyes. The boys crowded around in an awe-stricken way, and even his classmates and those with whom he was well acquainted looked at him with a certain respect he had never seen before.

He had never imagined such stiffness

6   Examination Day

It was plain that Fred and Charley had spread the news of their descent into the Pit, and of their battle with the Simpson clan and the Fishes. He heard the nine o'clock bell with feelings of relief, and passed into the school, a mark for admiring glances from all the boys. The girls, too, looked at him in a timid and fearful way – as they might have looked at Daniel when he came out of the lions' den, Joe thought, or at David after his battle with Goliath. It made him uncomfortable and painfully self-conscious, this hero-worshipping, and he wished heartily that they would look in some other direction for a change.

Soon they did look in another direction. While big sheets of foolscap were being distributed to every desk, Miss Wilson, the teacher (an austere-looking young woman who went through the world as though it were a refrigerator, and who, even on the warmest days in the classroom, was to be found with a shawl or cape about her shoulders), arose, and on the blackboard where all could see wrote the Roman numeral 'I.' Every eye, and there were fifty pairs of them, hung with expectancy upon her hand, and in the pause that followed the room was quiet as the grave.

Underneath the Roman numeral 'I' she wrote: '(*a*) *What were the laws of Draco?* (*b*) *Why did an Athenian orator say that they were written "not in ink, but in blood"?*'

Forty-nine heads bent down and forty-nine pens scratched lustily across as many sheets of foolscap. Joe's head alone remained up, and he regarded the blackboard with so bland a stare that Miss Wilson, glancing over her shoulder after having written 'II,' stopped to look at him. Then she wrote:

'(*a*) *How did the war between Athens and Megara, respecting the island of Salamis, bring about the reforms of Solon?* (*b*) *In what way did they differ from the laws of Draco?*'

She turned to look at Joe again. He was staring as blankly as ever.

'What is the matter, Joe?' she asked. 'Have you no paper?'

'Yes, I have, thank you,' he answered, and began moodily to sharpen a lead pencil.

He made a fine point to it. Then he made a very fine point. Then, and with infinite patience, he proceeded to make it very much finer. Several of his classmates raised their heads inquiringly at the noise. But he did not notice. He was too absorbed in his pencil-sharpening and in thinking thoughts far away from both pencil-sharpening and Greek history.

'Of course you all understand that the examination papers are to be written with ink.'

Miss Wilson addressed the class in general, but her eyes rested on Joe.

Just as it was about as fine as it could possibly be the point broke, and Joe began over again.

'I am afraid, Joe, that you annoy the class,' Miss Wilson said in final desperation.

He put the pencil down, closed the knife with a snap, and returned to his blank staring at the blackboard. What did he know about Draco? or Solon? or the rest of the Greeks? It was a flunk, and that was all there was to it. No need for him to look at the rest of the questions, and even if he did know the answers to two or three, there was no use in writing them down. It would not prevent the flunk. Besides, his arm hurt him too much to write. It hurt his eyes to look at the blackboard, and his eyes hurt even when they were closed; and it seemed positively to hurt him to think.

So the forty-nine pens scratched on in a race after Miss Wilson, who was covering the blackboard with question after question; and he listened to the scratching, and watched the questions growing under her chalk, and was very miserable indeed. His head seemed whirling around. It ached inside and was sore outside, and he did not seem to have any control of it at all.

He was beset with memories of the Pit, like scenes from some monstrous nightmare, and, try as he would, he could not dispel them. He would fix his mind and eyes on Miss Wilson. She was now sitting at her desk, and even as he looked at her the face of Brick Simpson, impudent and pugnacious, would arise before him. It was of no use. He felt sick and sore and tired and worthless. There was nothing to be done but flunk. And when, after an age of waiting, the papers were collected, his went in a blank, save for his name, the name of the examination, and the date, which were written across the top.

After a brief interval, more papers were given out, and the examination in arithmetic began. He did not trouble himself to look at the questions. Ordinarily he might have pulled through such an examination, but in his present state of mind and body he knew it was impossible. He contented himself with burying his face in his hands and hoping for the noon hour. Once, lifting his eyes to the clock, he caught Bessie looking anxiously at him across the room from the girls' side. This but added to his discomfort. Why was she bothering him? No need for her to trouble. She was bound to pass. Then why couldn't she leave him alone? So he gave her a particularly glowering look and buried his face in his hands again. Nor did he lift it till the twelve-o'clock gong rang, when he handed in a second blank paper and passed out with the boys.

Fred and Charley and he usually ate lunch in a corner of the yard which they had arrogated to themselves; but this day, by some remarkable coincidence, a score of other boys had elected to eat their lunches on the same spot. Joe surveyed them with disgust. In his present condition he did not feel inclined to receive hero worship. His head ached too much, and he was troubled over his failure in the examinations; and there were more to come in the afternoon.

He was angry with Fred and Charley. They were chattering like magpies over the adventures of the night (in which, however, they did not fail to give him chief credit), and they conducted themselves in quite a patronising fashion toward their awed and admiring school-mates. But every attempt to make Joe talk was a failure. He grunted and gave short answers, and said 'yes' and 'no' to questions asked with the intention of drawing him out.

He was longing to get away somewhere by himself, to throw himself down some place on the green grass and forget his aches and pains and troubles. He got up to go and find such a place, and found half a dozen of his following tagging after him. He wanted to turn around and scream at them to leave him alone, but his pride restrained him. A great wave of disgust and despair swept over him, and then an idea flashed through his mind. Since he was sure to flunk in his examinations, why endure the afternoon's torture, which could not but be worse than the morning's? And on the impulse of the moment he made up his mind.

He walked straight on to the school yard gate and passed out. Here his worshippers halted in wonderment, but he kept on to the corner and out of sight. For some time he wandered along aimlessly, till he came to the tracks of a cable road. A downtown car happening to stop to let off passengers, he stepped aboard and ensconced himself in an outside corner seat. The next thing he was aware of, the car was swinging around on its turntable and he was hastily scrambling off. The big ferry building stood before him. Seeing and hearing nothing, he had been carried through the heart of the business section of San Francisco.

He glanced up at the tower clock on top of the ferry building. It was ten minutes after one – time enough to catch the quarter-past-one boat. That decided him, and without the least idea in the world as to where he was going, he paid ten cents for a ticket, passed through the gate, and was soon speeding across the bay to the pretty city of Oakland.

In the same aimless and unwitting fashion, he found himself, an hour later, sitting on the stringpiece of the Oakland city wharf and leaning his aching head against a friendly timber. From where he sat he could look down upon the decks of a number of small sailing craft. Quite a crowd of curious idlers had collected to look at them, and Joe found himself growing interested.

There were four boats, and from where he sat he could make out their names. The one directly beneath him had the name *Ghost* painted in large green letters on its stern. The other three, which lay beyond, were called respectively *La Caprice*, the *Oyster Queen*, and the *Flying Dutchman*.

Each of these boats had cabins built amidships, with short stove-pipes projecting through the roofs, and from the pipe of the *Ghost* smoke was ascending. The cabin doors were open and the roof slide pulled back, so that Joe could look inside and observe the inmate, a young fellow of nineteen or twenty who was engaged just then in cooking. He was clad in long sea boots which reached the hips, blue overalls, and dark woollen shirt. The sleeves, rolled back to the elbows, disclosed sturdy, sun-bronzed arms, and when the young fellow looked up his face proved to be equally bronzed and tanned.

The aroma of coffee arose to Joe's nose, and from a light iron pot came the unmistakable smell of beans nearly done. The cook placed a frying pan on the stove, wiped it around with a piece of suet when it had heated, and tossed in a thick chunk of beefsteak. While he worked he talked with a companion on deck, who was busily engaged in filling a bucket overside and flinging the salt water over heaps of oysters that lay on the deck. This completed, he covered the oysters with wet sacks, and went into the cabin, where a place was set for him on a tiny table, and where the cook served the dinner and joined him in eating it.

All the romance of Joe's nature stirred at the sight. That was life. They were living, and gaining their living, out in the free open, under the sun and sky, with the sea rocking beneath them, and the wind blowing on them, or the rain falling on them, as the chance might be. Each day and every day he sat in a room, pent up with fifty more of his kind, racking his brains and cramming dry husks of knowledge, while they were doing all this, living glad and careless and happy, rowing boats and sailing, and cooking their own food, and certainly meeting with adventures such as one only dreams of in the crowded schoolroom.

Joe sighed. He felt that he was made for this sort of life and not for the life of a scholar. As a scholar he was undeniably a failure. He had flunked in his examinations, while at that very moment, he knew, Bessie was going triumphantly home, her last examination over and done, and with credit. Oh, it was not to be borne! His father was wrong in sending him to school. That might be well enough for boys who were inclined to study, but it was manifest that he was not so inclined. There were more careers in life than that of the schools. Men had gone down to the sea in the lowest capacity, and risen in greatness, and owned great fleets, and done great deeds, and left their names on the pages of time. And why not he, Joe Bronson?

He closed his eyes and felt immensely sorry for himself; and when he opened his eyes again he found that he had been asleep, and that the sun was sinking fast.

It was after dark when he arrived home, and he went straight to his room and to bed without meeting anyone. He sank down between the cool sheets with a sigh of satisfaction at the thought that, come what would, he need no longer worry about his history. Then another and unwelcome thought obtruded itself, and he knew that the next school term would come, and that six months thereafter, another examination in the same history awaited him.

7　Father and Son

On the following morning, after breakfast, Joe was summoned to the library by his father, and he went in almost with a feeling of gladness that the suspense of waiting was over. Mr Bronson was standing by the window. A great chattering of sparrows outside seemed to have attracted his attention. Joe joined him in looking out, and saw a fledgeling sparrow on the grass, tumbling ridiculously about in its efforts to stand on its feeble baby legs. It had fallen from the nest in the rosebush that climbed over the window, and the two parent sparrows were wild with anxiety over its plight.

'It's a way young birds have,' Mr Bronson remarked, turning to Joe with a serious smile, 'and I dare say you are on the verge of a somewhat similar predicament, my boy,' he went on. 'I am afraid things have reached a crisis, Joe. I have watched it coming on for a year now – your poor scholarship, your carelessness and inattention, your constant desire to be out of the house and away in search of adventures of one sort or another.'

He paused, as though expecting a reply; but Joe remained silent.

'I have given you plenty of liberty. I believe in liberty. The finest souls grow in such soil. So I have not hedged you in with endless rules and irksome restrictions. I have asked little of you, and you have come and gone pretty much as you pleased. In a way, I have put you on your honour, made you largely your own master, trusting to your sense of right to restrain you from going wrong and at least to keep you up in your studies. And you have failed me. What do you want me to do? Set you certain bounds and time limits? Keep a watch over you? Compel you by main strength to go through your books?

'I have here a note,' Mr Bronson said after another pause, in which he picked up an envelope from the table and drew forth a written sheet.

Joe recognized the stiff and uncompromising scrawl of Miss Wilson, and his heart sank.

His father began to read:

Listlessness and carelessness have characterised his term's work, so that when the examinations came he was wholly unprepared. In neither history nor arithmetic did he attempt to answer a question, passing in his papers perfectly blank. These examinations took place in the morning. In the afternoon he did not take the trouble even to appear for the remainder.

Mr Bronson ceased reading and looked up.

'Where were you in the afternoon?' he asked.

'I went across on the ferry to Oakland,' Joe answered, not caring to offer his aching head and body in extenuation.

'That is what is called "playing hooky," is it not?'

'Yes, sir,' Joe answered.

'The night before the examinations, instead of studying, you saw fit to wander away and involve yourself in a disgraceful fight with hoodlums. I did not say anything at the time. In my heart I think I might almost have forgiven you that, if you had done well in your schoolwork.'

Joe had nothing to say. He knew that there was his side to the story, but he felt that his father did not understand, and that there was little use of telling him.

'The trouble with you, Joe, is carelessness and lack of concentration. What you need is what I have not given you, and that is rigid discipline. I have been debating for some time upon the advisability of sending you to some military school, where your tasks will be set for you, and what you do every moment in the twenty-four hours will be determined for you——'

'Oh, father, you don't understand, you can't understand!' Joe broke forth at last. 'I try to study – I honestly try to study; but somehow – I don't know how – I can't study. Perhaps I am a failure. Perhaps I am not made for study. I want to go out into the world. I want to see life – to live. I don't want any military academy; I'd sooner go to sea – anywhere I can do something and be something.'

Mr Bronson looked at him kindly. 'It is only through study that you can hope to do something and be something in the world,' he said.

Joe threw up his hand with a gesture of despair.

'I know how you feel about it,' Mr Bronson went on; 'but you are only a boy, very much like that young sparrow we were watching. If at home you have not sufficient control over yourself to study, then away from home, out in the world which you think is calling you, you will likewise not have sufficient control over yourself to do the work of that world.

'But I am willing, Joe, I am willing, after you have finished high school and before you go into the university, to let you out into the world for a time.'

'Let me go now?' Joe asked impulsively.

'No; it is too early. You haven't your wings yet. You are too unformed, and your ideas and standards are not yet thoroughly fixed.'

'But I shall not be able to study,' Joe threatened. 'I know I shall not be able to study.'

Mr Bronson consulted his watch and arose to go. 'I have not made up my mind yet,' he said. 'I do not know what I shall do – whether I shall give you another trial at the public school or send you to a military academy.'

He stopped a moment at the door and looked back. 'But remember this, Joe,' he said. 'I am not angry with you; I am more grieved and hurt. Think it over, and tell me this evening what you intend to do.'

His father passed out, and Joe heard the front door close after him. He leaned back in the big easy chair and closed his eyes. A military school! He feared such an institution as the animal fears a trap. No, he would certainly never go to such a place. And as for public school – He sighed deeply at the thought of it. He was given till evening to make up his mind as to what he intended to do. Well, he knew what he would do, and he did not have to wait till evening to find it out.

He got up with a determined look on his face, put on his hat, and went out the front door. He would show his father that he could do his share of the world's work, he thought as he walked along – he would show him.

By the time he reached the school he had his whole plan worked out definitely. Nothing remained but to put it through. It was the noon hour, and he passed in to his room and packed up his books unnoticed. Coming out through the yard, he encountered Fred and Charley.

'What's up?' Charley asked.

'Nothing,' Joe grunted.

What are you doing there?'

'Taking my books home, of course. What did you suppose I was doing?'

'Come, come,' Fred interposed. 'Don't be so mysterious. I don't see why you can't tell us what has happened.'

'You'll find out soon enough,' Joe said significantly – more significantly than he had intended.

And, for fear that he might say more, he turned his back on his astonished chums and hurried away. He went straight home and to his room, where he busied himself at once with putting everything in order. His clothes he hung carefully away, changing the suit he had on for an older one. From his bureau he selected a couple of changes of underclothing, a couple of cotton shirts, and half a dozen pairs of socks. To these he added as many handkerchiefs, a comb, and a toothbrush.

When he had bound the bundle in stout wrapping paper he contemplated it with satisfaction. Then he went over to his desk and took from a small inner compartment his savings for some months, which amounted to several dollars. This sum he had been keeping for the Fourth of July, but he thrust it into his pocket with hardly a regret. Then he pulled a writing pad over to him, sat down and wrote:

Don't look for me. I am a failure and I am going away to sea. Don't worry about me. I am all right and able to take care of myself. I shall come back some day, and then you will all be proud of me. Goodbye, papa, and mama, and Bessie.

JOE

This he left lying on his desk where it could easily be seen. He tucked the bundle under his arm, and, with a last farewell look at the room, stole out.

8 'Frisco Kid and the New Boy

'Frisco Kid was discontented – discontented and disgusted; though this would have seemed impossible to the boys who fished from the dock above and envied him mightily. He frowned, got up from where he had been sunning himself on top of the *Dazzler*'s cabin, and kicked off his heavy rubber boots. Then he stretched himself on the narrow side deck and dangled his feet in the cool salt water.

'Now, that's freedom,' thought the boys who watched him. Besides, those long sea boots, reaching the hips and buckled to the leather strap about the waist, held a strange and wonderful fascination for them. They did not know that 'Frisco Kid did not possess such things as shoes; that the boots were an old pair of Pete Le Maire's and were three sizes too large for him; nor could they guess how uncomfortable they were to wear on a hot summer day.

The cause of 'Frisco Kid's discontent was those very boys who sat on the stringpiece and admired him; but his disgust was the result of quite another event. Further, the *Dazzler* was short one in its crew, and he had to do more work than was justly his share. He did not mind the cooking, nor the washing down of the decks and the pumping; but when it came to the paint scrubbing and dishwashing, he rebelled. He felt that he had earned the right to be exempt from such scullion work. That was all the green boys were fit for; while he could make or take in sail, lift anchor, steer, and make landings.

'Stan' from un'er!' Pete Le Maire, captain of the *Dazzler* and lord and master of 'Frisco Kid, threw a bundle into the cockpit and came aboard by the starboard rigging.

'Come! Queeck!' he shouted to the boy who owned the bundle, and who now hesitated on the dock. It was a good fifteen feet to the deck of the sloop, and he could not reach the steel stay by which he must descend.

'Now! One, two, three!' the Frenchman counted good-naturedly, after the manner of all captains when their crews are shorthanded.

The boy swung his body into space and gripped the rigging. A moment later he struck the deck, his hands tingling warmly from the friction.

'Kid, dis is ze new sailor. I make your acquaintance.' Pete smirked and bowed, and stood aside. 'Mistaire Sho Bronson,' he added as an afterthought.

The two boys regarded each other silently for a moment. They were evidently about the same age, though the stranger looked the heartier and the stronger of the two. 'Frisco Kid put out his hand, and they shook.

'So you're thinking of tackling the water, eh?' he asked.

Joe Bronson nodded, and glanced curiously about him before answering. 'Yes; I think the Bay life will suit me for a while, and then, when I've got used to it, I'm going to sea in the forecastle.'

'In the what? In the *what*, did you say?'

'In the forecastle – the place where the sailors live,' he explained, flushing and feeling doubtful of his pronunciation.

'Oh, the fo'c'sle. Know anything about going to sea?'

'Yes – no; that is, except what I've read.'

'Frisco Kid whistled, turned on his heel in a lordly manner, and went into the cabin.

'Going to sea!' he remarked to himself as he built the fire and set about cooking supper. 'In the "forecastle," too – and thinks he'll like it!'

In the meantime Pete Le Maire was showing the newcomer about the sloop as though he were a guest. Such affability and charm did he display that 'Frisco Kid, popping his head up through the scuttle to call them to supper, nearly choked in his effort to suppress a grin.

Joe Bronson enjoyed that supper. The food was rough but good, and the smack of the salt air and the sea fittings around him gave zest to his appetite. The cabin was clean and snug, and, though not large, the accommodations surprised him. Every bit of space was utilised. The table swung to the centreboard case on hinges, so that when not in use it actually occupied almost no room at all. On either side, and partly under the deck, were two bunks. The blankets were rolled back, and they sat on the well-scrubbed bunk boards while they ate. A swinging sea lamp of brightly polished brass gave them light, which in the daytime could be obtained through the four deadeyes, or small round panes of heavy glass which were fitted into the walls of the cabin. On the side of the door were the stove and wood box, on the other the cupboard. The front end of the cabin was ornamented with a couple of rifles and a shotgun, while exposed by the rolled-back blankets of Pete's bunk was a cartridge-lined belt carrying a brace of revolvers.

It all seemed like a dream to Joe. Countless times he had imagined scenes somewhat similar to this; but here he was, right in the midst of it, and already it seemed as though he had known his two companions for years. Pete was smiling genially at him across the board. His was really a villainous countenance, but to Joe it seemed only 'weather-beaten.' 'Frisco Kid was describing to him, between mouthfuls, the last sou'easter the *Dazzler* had weathered, and Joe experienced an increasing awe for this boy who had lived so long upon the water and knew so much about it.

The captain, however, drank a glass of wine, and topped it off with a second and a third, and then, a vicious flush lighting his swarthy face, stretched out on top of his blankets, where he soon was snoring loudly.

'Better turn in and get a couple of hours' sleep,' 'Frisco Kid said kindly, pointing Joe's bunk out to him. 'We'll most likely be up the rest of the night.'

Joe obeyed, but he could not fall asleep so readily as the others. He lay with his eyes wide open, watching the hands of the alarm clock that hung in the cabin, and thinking how quickly event had followed event in the last twelve hours. Only that very morning he had been a schoolboy, and now he was a sailor, shipped on the *Dazzler*, and bound he knew not whither. His fifteen years increased to twenty at the thought of it, and he felt every inch a man – a sailorman at that. He wished Charley and Fred could see him now. Well, they would hear of it quick enough. He could see them talking it over, and the other boys crowding around. 'Who?' 'What! – Joe Bronson?' 'Yes, he's run away to sea. Used to chum with us, you know.'

Joe pictured the scene proudly. Then he softened at the thought of his mother worrying, but hardened again at the recollection of his father. Not that his father was not good and kind; but he did not understand boys, Joe thought. That was where the trouble lay. Only that morning he had said that the world wasn't a playground, and that the boys who thought it was were liable to make sore mistakes and be glad to get home again. Well, *he* knew that there was plenty of hard work and rough experience in the world; but *he* also thought boys had some rights and should be allowed to do a lot of things without being questioned. He'd show him he could take care of himself; and anyway, he could write home after he got settled down to his new life.

A skiff grazed the side of the *Dazzler* softly and interrupted his reveries. He wondered why he had not heard the sound of the rowlocks. Then two men jumped over the cockpit rail and came into the cabin.

'Bli' me, if 'ere they ain't snoozin',' said the first of the newcomers, deftly rolling 'Frisco Kid out of his blankets with one hand and reaching for the wine bottle with the other.

Pete put his head up on the other side of the centreboard, his eyes heavy with sleep, and made them welcome.

'' 'Oo's this?' asked 'the Cockney,' as 'Frisco Kid called him, smacking his lips over the wine and rolling Joe out upon the floor. 'Passenger?'

'No, no,' Pete made haste to answer. 'Ze new sailorman. Vaire good boy.'

'Good boy or not, he's got to keep his tongue a-tween his teeth,' growled the second newcomer, who had not yet spoken, glaring fiercely at Joe.

'I say,' queried the other man, '' 'ow does 'e whack up on the loot? I 'ope as me an' Bill 'ave a square deal.'

'Ze *Dazzler* she take one share – what you call – one third; den we split ze rest in five shares. Five men, five shares. Vaire good.'

It was all Greek to Joe, except he knew that he was in some way the cause of the quarrel. In the end Pete had his way, and the newcomers gave in after much grumbling. After they had drunk their coffee all hands went on deck.

'Just stay in the cockpit an' keep out of their way,' 'Frisco Kid whispered to Joe. 'I'll teach you the ropes an' everything when we ain't in a hurry.'

Joe's heart went out to him in sudden gratitude, for the strange feeling came to him that, of those on board, to 'Frisco Kid, and to 'Frisco Kid only, could he look for help in time of need. Already a dislike for Pete was growing up within him. Why, he could not say – he just simply felt it. A creaking of blocks for'ard, and the huge mainsail loomed above him in the night. Bill cast off the bowline. The Cockney followed with the stern. 'Frisco Kid gave her the jib as Pete jammed up the tiller, and the *Dazzler* caught the breeze, heeling over for mid-channel. Joe heard some talking in low tones of not putting up the side lights, and of keeping a sharp lookout, but all he could comprehend was that some law of navigation was being violated.

The water-front lights of Oakland began to slip past. Soon the stretches of docks and the shadowy ships began to be broken by dim sweeps of marshland, and Joe knew that they were heading out for San Francisco Bay. The wind was blowing from the north in mild squalls, and the *Dazzler* cut noiselessly through the landlocked water.

'Where are we going?' Joe asked the Cockney, in an endeavour to be friendly and at the same time satisfy his curiosity.

'Oh, my pardner 'ere, Bill – we're goin' to take a cargo from 'is factory,' that worthy airily replied.

Joe thought he was rather a funny-looking individual to own a factory; but conscious that stranger things yet might be found in this new world he was entering, he said nothing. He had already exposed himself to 'Frisco Kid in the matter of his pronunciation of 'fo'c'sle,' and he had no desire further to show his ignorance.

A little after that he was sent in to blow out the cabin lamp. The

The Waterfront lights of Oakland began to slip past

Dazzler tacked about and began to work in toward the north shore. Everybody kept silent, save for occasional whispered questions and answers which passed between Bill and the Captain. Finally the sloop was run into the wind and the jib and mainsail lowered cautiously.

'Short hawse, you know,' Pete whispered to 'Frisco Kid, who went for'ard and dropped the anchor, paying out the slightest quantity of slack.

The *Dazzler*'s skiff was brought alongside, as was also the small boat the two strangers had come aboard in.

'See that that cub don't make a fuss,' Bill commanded in an undertone, as he joined his partner in his own boat.

'Can you row?' 'Frisco Kid asked as they got into the other boat. Joe nodded his head. 'Then take these oars, and don't make a racket.'

'Frisco Kid took the second pair, while Pete steered. Joe noticed that the oars were muffled with sennit, and that even the rowlock sockets were protected by leather. It was impossible to make a noise except by a mis-stroke, and Joe had learned to row on Lake Merrit well enough to avoid that. They followed in the wake of the first boat, and glancing aside, he saw they were running along the length of a pier which jutted out from the land. A couple of ships, with riding lanterns burning brightly, were moored to it, but they kept just beyond the edge of the light. He stopped rowing at the whispered command of 'Frisco Kid. Then the boats grounded like ghosts on a tiny beach, and they clambered out.

Joe followed the men, who picked their way carefully up a twenty-foot bank. At the top he found himself on a narrow railway track which ran between huge piles of rusty scrap iron. These piles, separated by tracks, extended in every direction, he could not tell how far, though in the distance he could see the vague outlines of some great factorylike building. The men began to carry loads of the iron down to the beach, and Pete, gripping him by the arm and again warning him to not make any noise, told him to do likewise. At the beach they turned their loads over to 'Frisco Kid, who loaded them, first in one skiff and then in the other. As the boats settled under the weight, he kept pushing them farther and farther out, in order that they should keep clear of the bottom.

Joe worked away steadily, though he could not help marvelling at the queerness of the whole business. Why should there be such a mystery about it, and why such care taken to maintain silence? He had just begun to ask himself these questions, and a horrible suspicion was forming itself in his mind, when he heard the hoot of an owl from the direction of the beach. Wondering at an owl being in so unlikely a place, he stooped to gather a fresh load of iron. But suddenly a man sprang out of the gloom, flashing a dark lantern full upon him. Blinded by the light, he staggered back. Then a revolver in the man's hand went off. All Joe realised was that he was being shot at, while his legs manifested an overwhelming desire to get away. Even if he had so wished, he could not very well have stayed to explain to the excited man with the smoking revolver. So he took to his heels for the beach, colliding with another man with a dark lantern who came running around the end of one of the piles of iron. This second man quickly regained his feet, and peppered away at Joe as he flew down the bank.

He dashed out into the water for the boat. Pete at the bow oars and 'Frisco Kid at the stroke had the skiff's nose pointed seaward and were calmly awaiting his arrival. They had their oars all ready for the start, but they held them quietly at rest, notwithstanding that both men on the bank had begun to fire at them. The other skiff lay closer inshore, partially aground. Bill was trying to shove it off, and was calling on the Cockney to lend a hand; but that gentleman had lost his head completely, and came floundering through the water hard after Joe. No sooner had Joe climbed in over the stern than he followed him. This extra weight on the stern of the heavily loaded craft nearly swamped them; as it was, a dangerous quantity of water was shipped. In the meantime the men on the bank had reloaded their pistols and opened fire again, this time with better aim. The alarm had spread. Voices and cries could be heard from the ships on the pier, along which men were running. In the distance a police whistle was being frantically blown.

'Get out!' 'Frisco Kid shouted. 'You ain't a-going to sink us if I know it. Go and help your pardner!'

But the Cockney's teeth were chattering with fright, and he was too unnerved to move or speak.

'T'row ze crazy man out!' Pete ordered from the bow. At this moment a bullet shattered an oar in his hand, and he coolly proceeded to ship a spare one.

'Give us a hand, Joe,' 'Frisco Kid commanded.

Joe understood, and together they seized the terror-stricken creature and flung him overboard. Two or three bullets splashed about him as he came to the surface just in time to be picked up by Bill, who had at last succeeded in getting clear.

'Now,' Pete called, and a few strokes into the darkness quickly took them out of the zone of fire.

So much water had been shipped that the light skiff was in danger of sinking at any moment. While the other two rowed, and by the Frenchman's orders, Joe began to throw out the iron. This saved them for the time being; but just as they swept alongside the *Dazzler* the skiff lurched, shoved a side under, and turned turtle, sending the remainder of the iron to the bottom. Joe and 'Frisco Kid came up side by side, and together they clambered aboard with the skiff's painter in two. Pete had already arrived, and now helped them out.

By the time they had canted the water out of the swamped boat, Bill and his partner appeared on the scene. All hands worked rapidly, and almost before Joe could realise, the mainsail and jib had been hoisted, the anchor broken out, and the *Dazzler* was leaping down the channel. Off a bleak piece of marshland, Bill and the Cockney said goodbye and cast loose in the skiff. Pete, in the cabin, bewailed their bad luck in various languages, and sought consolation in the wine bottle.

The wind freshened as they got clear of the land, and soon the *Dazzler* was heeling it with her lee deck buried and the water churning by halfway up the cockpit rail. Side lights had been hung out. 'Frisco Kid was steering, and by his side sat Joe, pondering over the events of the night.

He could no longer blind himself to the facts. His mind was in a

whirl of apprehension. If he had done wrong, he reasoned, he had done
it through ignorance; and he did not feel shame for the past so much as
he did fear of the future. His companions were thieves and robbers –
the Bay pirates, of whose unlawful deeds he had heard vague tales.
And here he was, right in the midst of them, already possessing
information which could send them to state's prison. This very fact, he
knew, would force them to keep a sharp watch upon him and so lessen
his chances of escape. But escape he would, at the very first
opportunity.

At this point his thoughts were interrupted by a sharp squall,
which hurled the *Dazzler* over till the sea rushed inboard. 'Frisco Kid
luffed quickly, at the same time slacking off the mainsheet. Then,
singlehanded – for Pete remained below, and Joe sat still looking idly
on – he proceeded to reef down.

10 Joe Loses Liberty and Finds a Friend

Joe was in a predicament, and a very tantalising one at that. A few minutes of hard rowing would bring him to the beach and to safety; but on that beach, for some unaccountable reason, stood a United States soldier who persisted in firing at him.

When Joe saw the gun aimed at him for the third time, he backed water hastily. As a result the skiff came to a standstill, and the soldier, lowering his rifle, regarding him intently.

'I want to come ashore! Important!' Joe shouted out to him.

The man in uniform shook his head.

'But it's important, I tell you! Won't you let me come ashore?'

He took a hurried look in the direction of the *Dazzler*. The shots had evidently awakened Pete; for the mainsail had been hoisted, and as he looked he saw the anchor broken out and the jib flung to the breeze.

'Can't land here!' the soldier shouted back. 'Smallpox!'

'But I must!' he cried, choking down a half sob and preparing to row.

'Then I'll shoot,' was the cheering response, and the rifle came to shoulder again.

Joe thought rapidly. The island was large. Perhaps there were no soldiers farther on, and if he only once got ashore he did not care how quickly they captured him. He might catch the smallpox, but even that was better than going back to the Bay pirates. He whirled the skiff half about to the right, and threw all his strength against the oars. The cove was quite wide, and the nearest point which he must go around a good distance away. Had he been more of a sailor he would have gone in the exerted their puny strength in the face of violent nature, and together they had outwitted her.

He came back to where his companion stood at the tiller steering, and he felt proud of him and of himself. And when he read the unspoken praise in 'Frisco Kid's eyes he blushed like a girl at her first compliment. But the next instant the thought flashed across him that this boy was a thief, a common thief, and he instinctively recoiled. His whole life had been sheltered from the harsher things of the world. His reading, which had been of the best, had laid a premium upon honesty and uprightness, and he had learned to look with abhorrence upon the criminal classes. So he drew a little away from 'Frisco Kid and remained silent. But 'Frisco Kid, devoting all his energies to the handling of the sloop, had no time in which to remark this sudden change of feeling on the part of his companion.

Yet there was one thing Joe found in himself that surprised him. While the thought of 'Frisco Kid being a thief was repulsive to him, 'Frisco Kid himself was not. Instead of feeling an honest desire to shun him, he felt drawn toward him. He could not help liking him, though he knew not why. Had he been a little older he would have understood that it was the lad's good qualities which appealed to him – his coolness and self-reliance, his manliness and bravery, and a certain kindliness and sympathy in his nature. As it was, he thought it his own natural badness which prevented him from disliking 'Frisco Kid, and while he felt shame at his own weakness, he could not smother the sort of regard which he felt growing up for this common thief, this Bay pirate.

'Take in two or three feet on the skiff's painter,' commanded 'Frisco Kid, who had an eye for everything.

The skiff was towing with too long a painter, and was behaving very badly. Every once in a while it would hold back till the towrope tautened, then coming leaping ahead and sheering and dropping slack till it threatened to shove its nose under the huge whitecaps which roared hungrily on every hand. Joe climbed over the cockpit rail upon the slippery afterdeck, and made his way to the bitt to which the skiff was fastened.

'Be careful,' 'Frisco Kid warned, as a heavy puff struck the

Dazzler and careened her dangerously over on her side. 'Keep one turn round the bitt, and heave in on it when the painter slacks.'

It was ticklish work for a greenhorn. Joe threw off all the turns save the last, which he held with one hand, while with the other he attempted to bring in on the painter. But at that instant it tightened with a tremendous jerk, the boat sheering sharply into the crest of a heavy sea. The rope slipped from his hands and began to fly out over the stern. He clutched it frantically, and was dragged after it over the sloping deck.

'Let her go! Let her go!' 'Frisco Kid roared.

Joe let go just as he was on the verge of going overboard, and the skiff dropped rapidly astern. He glanced in a shamefaced way at his companion, expecting to be sharply reprimanded for his awkwardness. But 'Frisco Kid smiled good-naturedly.

'That's all right,' he said. 'No bones broke, and nobody overboard. Better to lose a boat than a man any day. That's what I say. Besides, I shouldn't have sent you out there. And there's no harm done. We can pick it up all right. Go in and drop some more centreboard – a couple of feet – and then come out and do what I tell you. But don't be in a hurry. Take it easy and sure.'

Joe dropped the centreboard, and returned, to be stationed at the jib sheet.

'Hard a-lee!' 'Frisco Kid cried, throwing the tiller down and following it with his body. 'Cast off! That's right! Now lend a hand on the mainsheet!'

Together, hand over hand, they came in on the reefed mainsail. Joe began to warm up with the work. The *Dazzler* turned on her heel like a race horse and swept into the wind, her canvas snarling and her sheets slatting like hail.

'Draw down the jib sheet!'

Joe obeyed, and the headsail, filling, forced her off on the other tack. This manœuvre had turned Pete's bunk from the lee to the weather side, and rolled him out on the cabin floor, where he lay in a drunken stupor.

'Frisco Kid, with his back against the tiller, and holding the sloop off that it might cover their previous course, looked at him with an expression of disgust, and muttered: 'The dog! We could well go to the bottom, for all he'd care or do!'

Twice they tacked, trying to go over the same ground, and then Joe discovered the skiff bobbing to windward in the starlit darkness.

'Plenty of time,' 'Frisco Kid cautioned, shooting the *Dazzler* into the wind toward it and gradually losing headway.

'Now!'

Joe leaned over the side, grasped the trailing painter, and made it fast to the bitt. Then they tacked ship again and started on their way. Joe still felt sore over the trouble he had caused, but 'Frisco Kid quickly put him at ease.

'Oh, that's nothing,' he said. 'Everybody does that when they're beginning. Now, some men forget all about the trouble they had in learning, and get mad when a greeny makes a mistake. I never do. Why, I remember——'

And here he told Joe of many of the mishaps which fell to him when, as a little lad, he first went on the water, and of some of the severe punishments for the same which were measured out to him. He had passed the running end of a lanyard over the tiller neck, and, as they talked, they sat side by side and close against each other, in the shelter of the cockpit.

'What place is that?' Joe asked as they flew by a lighthouse perched on a rocky headland.

'Goat Island. They've got a naval training station for boys over on the other side, and a torpedo magazine. There's jolly good fishing, too – rock cod. We'll pass to the lee of it and make across and anchor in the shelter of Angel Island. There's a quarantine station there. Then, when Pete gets sober, we'll know where he wants to go. You can turn in now and get some sleep. I can manage all right.'

Joe shook his head. There had been too much excitement for him to feel in the least like sleeping. He could not bear to think of it, with the *Dazzler* leaping and surging along, and shattering the seas into clouds of spray on her weather bow. His clothes had half dried already, and he preferred to stay on deck and enjoy it. The lights of Oakland had dwindled till they made only a hazy flare against the sky; but to the south the San Francisco lights, topping hills and sinking into valleys, stretched miles upon miles. Starting from the great ferry building and passing on to Telegraph Hill, Joe was soon able to locate the principal places of the city. Somewhere over in that maze of light and shadow was the home of his father, and perhaps even now they were thinking and worrying about him; and over there his sister Bessie was sleeping cozily, to wake up in the morning and wonder why her brother Joe did not come down to breakfast. Joe shivered. It was almost morning. Then, slowly, his head drooped over on 'Frisco Kid's shoulder, and soon he was fast asleep.

'Come! Wake up! We're going into anchor.'

Joe roused with a start, bewildered at the unusual scene; for sleep had banished his troubles for the time being, and he knew not where he was. Then he remembered. The wind had dropped with the night. Beyond, the heavy aftersea was still rolling, but the *Dazzler* was creeping up in the shelter of a rocky island. The sky was clear, and the air had the snap and vigour of early morning about it. The rippling water was laughing in the rays of the sun, just shouldering above the eastern sky line. To the south lay Alcatraz Island, and from its gun-crowned heights a flourish of trumpets saluted the day. In the west the Golden Gate yawned between the Pacific Ocean and San Francisco Bay. A full-rigged ship, with her lightest canvas, even to the skysails, set, was coming slowly in on the flood tide.

It was a pretty sight. Joe rubbed the sleep from his eyes and remained gazing till 'Frisco Kid told him to go for'ard and make ready for dropping the anchor.

'Overhaul about fifty fathoms of chain,' he ordered, 'and then stand by.' He eased the sloop gently into the wind, at the same time casting off the jib sheet. 'Let go the jib halyards and come in on the downhaul!'

Joe had seen the manœuvre performed the previous night, and so was able to carry it out with fair success.

'Now! Over with the mud hook! Watch out for turns! Lively, now!'

The chain flew out with startling rapidity, and brought the

Dazzler to rest. 'Frisco Kid went for'ard to help, and together they lowered the mainsail, furled it in shipshape manner, made all fast with the gaskets, and put the crutches under the main boom.

'Here's a bucket.' 'Frisco Kid passed him the article in question. 'Wash down the decks, and don't be afraid of the water, nor of the dirt, neither. Here's a broom. Give it what for, and have everything shining. When you get that done, bail out the skiff; she opened her seams a little last night. I'm going below to cook breakfast.'

The water was soon sloshing merrily over the deck, while the smoke pouring from the cabin stove carried a promise of good things to come. Time and again Joe lifted his head from his task to take in the scene. It was one to appeal to any healthy boy, and he was no exception. The romance of it stirred him strangely, and his happiness would have been complete could he have escaped remembering who and what his companions were. But the thought of this, and of Pete in his blearly, drunken sleep below, marred the beauty of the day. He had been unused to such things, and was shocked at the harsh reality of life. But instead of hurting him, as it might a lad of weaker nature, it had the opposite effect. It strengthened his desire to be clean and strong, and to not be ashamed of himself in his own eyes. He glanced about him and sighed. Why could not men be honest and true? It seemed too bad that he must go away and leave all this; but the events of the night were strong upon him, and he knew that in order to be true to himself he must escape.

At this juncture he was called to breakfast. He discovered that 'Frisco Kid was as good a cook as he was sailor, and made haste to do justice to the fare, There were mush and condensed milk, beefsteak and fried potatoes, and all topped off with good French bread, butter, and coffee. Pete did not join them, though 'Frisco Kid attempted a couple of times to rouse him. He mumbled and grunted, half opened his bleared eyes, then went to snoring again.

'Can't tell when he's going to get those spells,' 'Frisco Kid explained, when Joe, having finished washing the dishes, came on deck. 'Sometimes he won't get that way for a month, and others he won't be decent for a week at a stretch. Sometimes he's good-natured, and sometimes he's dangerous. So the best thing to do is to let him alone and keep out of his way. And don't cross him, for if you do there's liable to be trouble.'

'Come on, let's take a swim,' he added, abruptly changing the subject to one more agreeable. 'Can you swim?'

Joe nodded. 'What's that place?' he asked as he poised before diving, pointing toward a sheltered beach on the island, where there were several buildings and a large number of tents.

'Quarantine station. Lots of smallpox coming in now on the China steamers, and they make them go there till the doctors say they're safe to land. I tell you, they're strict about it, too. Why——'

Splash! Had 'Frisco Kid finished his sentence just then, instead of diving overboard, much trouble might have been saved to Joe. But he did not finish it, and Joe dived after him.

'I'll tell you what,' 'Frisco Kid suggested half an hour later, while they clung to the bobstay preparatory to climbing out. 'Let's catch a mess of fish for dinner, and then turn in and make up for the sleep we lost last night. What d' you say?'

They made a race to clamber aboard, but Joe was shoved over the side again. When he finally did arrive, the other lad had brought to light a pair of heavily leaded, large-hooked lines, and a mackerel keg of salt sardines.

'Bait,' he said. 'Just shove a whole one on. They're not a bit partic'lar. Swallow the bait, hook and all, and go – that's their caper. The fellow that don't catch first fish has to clean 'em.'

Both sinkers started on their long descent together, and seventy feet of line whizzed out before they came to rest. But at the instant his sinker touched the bottom Joe felt the struggling jerks of a hooked fish. As he began to haul in he glanced at 'Frisco Kid, and saw that he, too, had evidently captured a finny prize. The race between them was exciting. Hand over hand the wet lines flashed inboard; but 'Frisco Kid was more expert, and his fish tumbled into the cockpit first. Joe's followed an instant later – a three-pound rock cod. He was wild with joy. It was magnificent, the largest fish he had ever landed or ever seen landed. Over went the lines again, and up they came with two mates of the ones already captured. It was sport royal. Joe would have certainly continued till he had fished the Bay empty had not 'Frisco Kid persuaded him to stop.

'We've got enough for three meals now,' he said, 'so there's no use in having them spoil. Besides, the more you catch, the more you clean, and you'd better start in right away. I'm going to bed.'

Joe did not mind. In fact, he was glad he had not caught the first fish, for it helped out a little plan which had come to him while in swimming. He threw the last cleaned fish into a bucket of water, and glanced about him. The quarantine station was a bare half mile away, and he could make out a soldier pacing up and down at sentry duty on the beach. Going into the cabin, he listened to the heavy breathing of the sleepers. He had to pass so close to 'Frisco Kid to get his bundle of clothes that he decided not to take them. Returning outside, he carefully pulled the skiff alongside, got aboard with a pair of oars, and cast off.

At first he rowed very gently in the direction of the station, fearing the chance of noise if he made undue haste. But gradually he increased the strength of his strokes till he had settled down to the regular stride. When he had covered half the distance he glanced about. Escape was sure now, for he knew, even if he were discovered, that it would be impossible for the *Dazzler* to get under way and head him off before he made the land and the protection of that man who wore the uniform of Uncle Sam.

The report of a gun came to him from the shore, but his back was in that direction and he did not bother to turn around. A second report followed, and a bullet cut the water within a couple of feet of his oar blade. This time he did turn around. The soldier on the beach was levelling his rifle at him for a third shot.

9   Joe Tries Taking French Leave

The squall which had so nearly capsized the *Dazzler* was of short duration, but it marked the rising of the wind, and soon puff after puff was shrieking down upon them out of the north. The mainsail was spilling the wind, and slapping and thrashing about till it seemed it would tear itself to pieces. The sloop was rolling wildly in the quick sea which had come up. Everything was in confusion; but even Joe's untrained eye showed him that it was an orderly confusion. He could see that 'Frisco Kid knew just what to do, and just how to do it. As he watched him he learned a lesson, the lack of which has made failures of the lives of many men – *knowledge of one's own capacities*. 'Frisco Kid knew what he was able to do, and because of this he had confidence in himself. He was cool and self-possessed, working hurriedly but not carelessly. There was no bungling. Every reef point was drawn down to stay. Other accidents might occur, but the next squall, or the next forty squalls, would not carry one of these reef knots away.

He called Joe for'ard to help stretch the mainsail by means of swinging on the peak and throat halyards. To lie out on the long bowsprit and put a single reef in the jib was a slight task compared with what had been already accomplished; so a few moments later they were again in the cockpit. Under the other lad's directions, Joe flattened down the jib sheet, and, going into the cabin, let down a foot or so of centreboard. The excitement of the struggle had chased all unpleasant thoughts from his mind. Patterning after the other boy, he had retained his coolness. He had executed his orders without fumbling, and at the same time without undue slowness. Together they had other direction for the opposite point, and thus had the wind on his pursuers. As it was, the *Dazzler* had a beam wind in which to overtake him.

It was nip and tuck for a while. The breeze was light and not very steady, so sometimes he gained and sometimes they. Once it freshened till the sloop was within a hundred yards of him, and then it dropped suddenly flat, the *Dazzler*'s big mainsail flapping idly from side to side.

'Ah! you steal ze skiff, eh?' Pete howled at him, running into the cabin for his rifle. 'I fix you! You come back queeck, or I kill you!' But he knew the soldier was watching them from the shore, and did not dare to fire, even over the lad's head.

Joe did not think of this, for he, who had never been shot at in all his previous life, had been under fire twice in the last twenty-four hours. Once more or less couldn't amount to much. So he pulled steadily away, while Pete raved like a wild man, threatening him with all manner of punishments once he laid hands upon him again. To complicate matters, 'Frisco Kid waxed mutinous.

'Just you shoot him and I'll see you hung for it, see if I don't,' he threatened. 'You'd better let him go. He's a good boy and all right, and not raised for the life you and I are leading.'

'You too, eh!' the Frenchman shrieked, beside himself with rage. 'Den I fix you, you rat!'

He made a rush for the boy, but 'Frisco Kid led him a lively chase from cockpit to bowsprit and back again. A sharp capful of wind arriving just then, Pete abandoned the one chase for the other. Springing to the tiller and slacking away on the mainsheet – for the wind favoured – he headed the sloop down upon Joe. The latter made one tremendous spurt, then gave up in despair and hauled in his oars. Pete let go the mainsheet, lost steerage way as he rounded up alongside the motionless skiff, and dragged Joe out.

'Keep mum,' 'Frisco Kid whispered to him while the irate Frenchman was busy fastening the painter. 'Don't talk back. Let him say all he wants to, and keep quiet. It'll be better for you.'

But Joe's Anglo-Saxon blood was up and he did not heed.

'Look here, Mr Pete, or whatever your name is,' he commenced, 'I give you to understand that I want to quit, and that I'm going to quit. So you'd better put me ashore at once. If you don't, I'll put you in prison, or my name's not Joe Bronson.'

'Frisco Kid waited the outcome fearfully. Pete was aghast. He was being defied aboard his own vessel, and by a boy. Never had such a thing been heard of. He knew he was committing an unlawful act in detaining him, while at the same time he was afraid to let him go with the information he had gathered concerning the sloop and its occupation. The boy had spoken the unpleasant truth when he said he could send him to prison. The only thing for him to do was to bully him.

'You will, eh?' His shrill voice rose wrathfully. 'Den you come too. You row ze boat last-a night – answer me dat! You steal ze iron – answer me dat! You run away – answer me dat! And den you say you put me in jail? Bah!'

'But I didn't know,' Joe protested.

'Ha, ha! Dat is funny. You tell dat to ze judge; mebbe him laugh, eh?'

'I say I didn't,' Joe reiterated manfully. 'I didn't know I'd shipped along with a lot of pirates and thieves.'

'Frisco Kid winced at this epithet, and had Joe been looking at him he would have seen him flush.

'And now that I do know,' he continued, 'I wish to be put ashore. I don't know anything about the law, but I do know right and wrong, and I'm willing to take my chance with any judge for whatever wrong I have done – with all the judges in the United States, for that matter. And that's more than you can say, Mr Pete.'

'You say dat, eh? Vaire good. But you are one big t'ief——'

'I'm not! Don't you dare call me that again!' Joe's face was pale, and he was trembling – but not with fear.

'T'ief!' the Frenchman taunted back.

'You lie!'

Joe had not been a boy among boys for nothing. He knew the penalty which attached itself to the words he had just spoken, and he

expected to receive it. So he was not overmuch surprised when he
picked himself up from the floor of the cockpit an instant later, his
head still ringing from a stiff blow between the eyes.

'Say dat one time more,' Pete bullied, his fist raised and prepared
to strike.

Tears of anger stood in Joe's eyes, but he was calm and in dead
earnest. 'When you say I am a thief, Pete, you lie. You can kill me, but
still I will say you lie.'

'No, you don't!' 'Frisco Kid had darted in like a wildcat,
preventing a second blow and shoving the Frenchman back across the
cockpit.

'You leave the boy alone,' he continued, suddenly unshipping and
arming himself with the heavy iron tiller, and standing between them.
'This thing's gone just about as far as it's going to go. You big fool,
can't you see the stuff the boy's made out of? He speaks true. He's
right, and he knows it, and you could kill him and he wouldn't give in.
There's my hand on it, Joe.' He turned and extended his hand to Joe,
who returned the grip. 'You've got spunk, and you're not afraid to
show it.'

Pete's mouth twisted itself in a sickly smile, but the evil gleam in
his eyes gave it the lie. He shrugged his shoulders and said: 'Ah! So? He
does not dee-sire dat I him call pet names. Ha, ha! It is only ze
sailorman play. Let us – what you call – forgive and forget, eh? Vaire
good; forgive and forget.'

He reached out his hand, but Joe refused to take it. 'Frisco Kid
nodded approval, while Pete, still shrugging his shoulders and
smiling, passed into the cabin.

'Slack off ze mainsheet,' he called out, 'and run down for Hunter's
Point. For one time I will cook ze dinner, and den you will say dat is ze
vaire good dinner. Ah! Pete is ze great cook!'

'That's the way he always does – gets real good and cooks when he
wants to make up,' 'Frisco Kid hazarded, slipping the tiller into the
rudderhead and obeying the order. 'But even then you can't trust
him.'

Joe nodded his head, but did not speak. He was in no mood for

'Slack off ze mainsheet and run down for Hunter's Point'

conversation. He was still trembling from the excitement of the last few moments, while deep down he questioned himself on how he had behaved, and found naught to be ashamed of.

The afternoon sea breeze had sprung up and was now rioting in from the Pacific. Angel Island was fast dropping astern, and the water front of San Francisco showing up, as the *Dazzler* ploughed along before it. Soon they were in the midst of the shipping, passing in and out among the vessels which had come from the uttermost ends of the earth. Later they crossed the fairway, where the ferry steamers, crowded with passengers, passed backward and forward between San Francisco and Oakland. One came so close that the passengers crowded to the side to see the gallant little sloop and the two boys in the cockpit. Joe gazed almost enviously at the row of down-turned faces. They all were going to their homes, while he – he was going he knew not whither, at the will of Pete Le Maire. He was half tempted to cry out for help; but the foolishness of such an act struck him, and he held his tongue. Turning his head, his eyes wandered along the smoky heights of the city, and he fell to musing on the strange ways of men and ships on the sea.

'Frisco Kid watched him from the corner of his eye, following his thoughts as accurately as though he spoke them aloud.

'Got a home over there somewhere?' he queried suddenly, waving his hand in the direction of the city.

Joe started, so correctly had his thought been anticipated. 'Yes,' he said simply.

'Tell us about it.'

Joe rapidly described his home, though forced to go into greater detail because of the curious questions of his companion. 'Frisco Kid was interested in everything, especially in Mrs Bronson and Bessie. Of the latter he could not seem to tire, and poured forth question after question concerning her. So peculiar and artless were some of them that Joe could hardly forbear to smile.

'Now tell me about your home,' he said, when he at last had finished.

'Frisco Kid seemed suddenly to harden, and his face took on a stern look which the other had never seen there before. He swung his foot idly to and fro, and lifted a dull eye to the main-peak blocks, with which, by the way, there was nothing the matter.

'Go ahead,' the other encouraged.

'I haven't no home.'

The four words left his mouth as though they had been forcibly ejected, and his lips came together after them almost with a snap.

Joe saw he had touched a tender spot, and strove to ease the way out of it again. 'Then the home you did have.' He did not dream that there were lads in the world who never had known homes, or that he had only succeeded in probing deeper.

'Never had none.'

'Oh!' His interest was aroused, and he now threw solicitude to the winds. 'Any sisters?'

'Nope.'

'Mother?'

'I was so young when she died that I don't remember her.'

'Father?'

'I never saw much of him. He went to sea – anyhow, he disappeared.'

'Oh!' Joe did not know what to say, and an oppressive silence, broken only by the churn of the *Dazzler*'s forefoot, fell upon them.

Just then Pete came out to relieve at the tiller, while they went in to eat. Both lads hailed his advent with feelings of relief, and the awkwardness vanished over the dinner, which was all their skipper had claimed it to be. Afterward 'Frisco Kid relieved Pete, and while he was eating, Joe washed up the dishes and put the cabin shipshape. Then they all gathered in the stern, where the captain strove to increase the general cordiality by entertaining them with descriptions of life among the pearl divers of the South Seas.

In this fashion the afternoon wore away. They had long since left San Francisco behind, rounded Hunter's Point, and were now skirting the San Mateo shore. Joe caught a glimpse, once, of a party of cyclists rounding a cliff on the San Bruno Road, and remembered the time when he had gone over the same ground on his own wheel. That was only a month or two before, but it seemed an age to him now, so much had there been to come between.

By the time supper had been eaten and the things cleared away, they were well down the Bay, off the marshes behind which Redwood City clustered. The wind had gone down with the sun, and the *Dazzler* was making but little headway, when they sighted a sloop bearing down upon them on the dying wind. 'Frisco Kid instantly named it as the *Reindeer*, to which Pete, after a deep scrutiny, agreed. He seemed greatly pleased at the meeting.

'Epont Nelson runs her,' 'Frisco Kid informed Joe. They've got something big down here and they're always after Pete to tackle it with them. He knows more about it, whatever it is.'

Joe nodded and looked at the approaching craft curiously. Though somewhat larger, it was built on about the same lines as the *Dazzler* – which meant, above everything else, that it was built for speed. The mainsail was so large that it was like that of a racing yacht, and it carried the points for no less than three reefs in case of rough weather. Aloft and on deck everything was in place; nothing was untidy or useless. From running gear to standing rigging, everything bore evidence of thorough order and smart seamanship.

The *Reindeer* came up slowly in the gathering twilight, and went to anchor not a biscuit toss away. Pete followed suit with the *Dazzler*, and then went in the skiff to pay them a visit. The two lads stretched themselves out on top of the cabin and awaited his return.

'Do you like the life?' Joe broke silence.

The other turned on his elbow. 'Well – I do, and then again I don't. The fresh air and the salt water, and all that, and the freedom – that's all right; but I don't like the – the——' he paused a moment, as though his tongue had failed in its duty, and then blurted out, 'the stealing.'

'Then why don't you quit it?' Joe liked the lad more than he dared confess, and he felt a sudden missionary zeal come upon him.

'I will, just as soon as I can turn my hand to something else.'

'But why not now?'

Now is the accepted time, was ringing in Joe's ears, and if the other wished to leave, it seemed a pity that he did not, and at once.

'Where can I go? What can I do? There's nobody in all the world to lend me a hand, just as there never has been. I tried it once, and learned my lesson too well to do it again in a hurry.'

'Well, when I get out of this I'm going home. Guess my father was right, after all. And I don't see – maybe – what's the matter with you going with me?' He said this last impulsively, without thinking, and 'Frisco Kid knew it.

'You don't know what you're talking about,' he answered. 'Fancy me going off with you! What'd your father say? And – and the rest? How would he think of me? And what'd he do?'

Joe felt sick at heart. He realised that in the spirit of the moment he had given an invitation which, on sober thought, he knew would be impossible to carry out. He tried to imagine his father receiving in his own house a stranger like 'Frisco Kid. No, that was not to be thought of. Then, forgetting his own plight, he fell to racking his brains for some other method by which 'Frisco Kid could get away from his present surroundings.

'He might turn me over to the police,' the other went on, 'and send me to a refuge. I'd die first, before I'd let that happen to me. And besides, Joe, I'm not of your kind, and you know it. Why, I'd be like a fish out of water, what with all the things I don't know. Nope; I guess I'll have to wait a little before I strike out. But there's only one thing for you to do, and that's go straight home. First chance I get, I'll land you, and then deal with Pete——'

'No, you don't,' Joe interrupted hotly. 'When I leave I'm not going to leave you in trouble on my account. So don't you try anything like that. I'll get away, never fear; and if I can figure it out, I want you to come along too – come along, anyway, and figure it out afterwards. What d' you say!'

'Frisco Kid shook his head, and, gazing up at the starlit heavens, wandered off into daydreams of the life he would like to lead, but from which he seemed inexorably shut out. The seriousness of life was striking deeper than ever into Joe's heart, and he lay silent, thinking hard. A mumble of heavy voices came to them from the *Reindeer*;

from the land the solemn notes of a church bell floated across the water; while the summer night wrapped them slowly in its warm darkness.

11   'Frisco Kid Tells His Story

After the conversation died away, the two lads lay upon the cabin for perhaps an hour.

Then, without saying a word, 'Frisco Kid went below and struck a light. Joe could hear him fumbling about, and a little later heard his own name called softly. On going into the cabin, he saw 'Frisco Kid sitting on the edge of the bunk, a sailor's ditty box on his knees, and in his hand a carefully folded page from a magazine.

'Does she look like this?' he asked, smoothing it out and turning it that the other might see.

It was a half-page illustration of two girls and a boy, grouped in an old-fashioned, roomy attic, and evidently holding a council of some sort. The girl who was talking faced the onlooker, while the backs of the two others were turned.

'Who?' Joe queried, glancing in perplexity from the picture to 'Frisco Kid's face.

'Like – like your sister – Bessie.' The name seemed reluctant to come from his lips.

Joe was nonplussed for the moment. He could see no bearing between the two in point, and, anyway, girls were rather silly creatures to waste one's time over. 'He's actually blushing,' he thought, regarding the soft glow on the other's cheeks. He felt an irresistible desire to laugh, but tried to smother it down.

'No, no, don't!' 'Frisco Kid cried, snatching the paper away and putting it back in the ditty box with shaking fingers. Then he added more slowly: 'I thought I – I kind of thought you would understand, and – and——'

His lips trembled and his eyes glistened with unwonted moistness as he turned hastily away.

The next instant Joe was by his side on the bunk, his arm around him. Prompted by some instinctive monitor, he had done it before he thought. A week before he could not have imagined himself in such an absurd situation – his arm around a boy! but now it seemed the most natural thing in the world. He did not comprehend, but he knew that, whatever it was, it was something that seemed of deep importance to his companion.

'Go ahead and tell us,' he urged. 'I'll understand.'

'No, you won't; you can't.'

'Yes – sure. Go ahead.'

'Frisco Kid choked and shook his head. 'I don't think I could, anyway. It's more the things I feel, and I don't know how to put them in words.' Joe's arm wrapped about him reassuringly, and he went on: 'Well, it's this way. You see, I don't know much about the land, and people, and homes, and I never had no brothers, or sisters, or playmates. All the time I didn't know it, but I was lonely – sort of missed them down in here somewheres.' He placed a hand over his breast to locate the seat of loss. 'Did you ever feel downright hungry? Well, that's just the way I used to feel, only a different kind of hunger, and me not knowing what it was. But one day, oh, a long time back, I got a-hold of a magazine, and saw a picture – that picture, with the two girls and the boy talking together. I thought it must be fine to be like them, and I got to thinking about the things they said and did, till it came to me all of a sudden like, and I knew that it was just loneliness was the matter with me.

'But, more than anything else, I got to wondering about the girl who looks out of the picture right at you. I was thinking about her all the time, and by and by she became real to me. You see, it was making believe, and I knew it all the time; and then again I didn't. Whenever I'd think of the men, and the work, and the hard life, I'd know it was make-believe; but when I'd think of her, it wasn't. I don't know; I can't explain it.'

Joe remembered all his own adventures which he had imagined on land and sea, and nodded. He at least understood that much.

'Of course it was all foolishness, but to have a girl like that for a friend seemed more like heaven to me than anything else I knew of. As I said, it was a long while back, and I was only a little kid. That's when Nelson gave me my name, and I've never been anything but 'Frisco Kid ever since. But the girl in the picture; I was always getting that picture out to look at her, and before long, if I wasn't square, why, I felt ashamed to look at her. Afterwards, when I was older, I came to look at it in another way. I thought, "Suppose, Kid, some day you were to meet a girl like that, what would she think of you? Could she like you? Could she be even the least bit of a friend to you?" And then I'd make up my mind to be better, to try and do something with myself so that she or any of her kind of people would not be ashamed to know me.

'That's why I learned to read. That's why I ran away. Nicky Perrata, a Greek boy, taught me my letters, and it wasn't till after I learned to read that I found out there was anything really wrong in Bay pirating. I'd been used to it ever since I could remember, and several people I knew made their living that way. But when I did find out, I ran away, thinking to quit it for good. I'll tell you about it sometime, and how I'm back at it again.

'Of course she seemed a real girl when I was a youngster, and even now she sometimes seems that way, I've thought so much about her. But while I'm talking to you it all clears up and she comes to me in this light; she stands just for – well, for a better cleaner life than this, and one I'd like to live; and if I could live it, why, I'd come to know that kind of girls, and their kind of people – your kind, that's what I mean. So I was wondering about your sister and you, and that's why – I don't know; I guess I was just wondering. But I suppose you know lots of girls like that, don't you?'

Joe nodded his head in token that he did.

'Then tell me about them; something – anything,' he added, as he noted the fleeting expression of doubt in the other's eyes.

'Oh, that's easy,' Joe began valiantly. To a certain extent he did understand the lad's hunger, and it seemed a simple enough task to satisfy him. 'To begin with, they're like – hem! – why, they're like – girls, just girls.' He broke off with a miserable sense of failure.

'Frisco Kid waited patiently, his face a study in expectancy.

Joe struggled vainly to marshal his ideas. To his mind, in quick succession, came the girls with whom he had gone to school, the sisters of the boys he knew, and those who were his sister's friends – slim girls and plump girls, tall girls and short girls, blue-eyed and brown-eyed, curly-haired, black-haired, golden-haired; in short, a regular procession of girls of all sorts and descriptions. But, to save himself, he could say nothing about them. Anyway, he'd never been a 'sissy,' and why should he be expected to know anything about them? 'All girls are alike,' he concluded desperately. 'They're just the same as the ones you know, Kid. Sure they are.'

'But I don't know any.'

Joe whistled. 'And never did?'

'Yes, one – Carlotta Gispardi. But she couldn't speak English; and she died. I don't care; though I never knew any, I seem to know as much about them as you do.'

'And I guess I know more about adventures all over the world than you do,' Joe retorted.

Both boys laughed. But a moment later Joe fell into deep thought. It had come upon him quite swiftly that he had not been duly grateful for the good things of life he did possess. Already home, father, and mother had assumed a greater significance to him; but he now found himself placing a higher personal value upon his sister, his chums and friends. He never had appreciated them properly, he thought, but henceforth – well, there would be a different tale to tell.

The voice of Pete hailing them put a finish to the conversation, for they both ran on deck.

'Get up ze mainsail, and break out ze hook!' he shouted. 'And den tail on to ze *Reindeer*! No side lights!'

'Come! Cast off those gaskets! Lively!' 'Frisco Kid ordered. 'Now lay onto the peak halyards – there, that rope; cast it off the pin. And don't hoist ahead of me. There! Make fast! We'll stretch it afterwards. Run aft and come in on the mainsheet! Shove the helm up!'

Under the sudden driving power of the mainsail, the *Dazzler* strained and tugged at her anchor like an impatient horse, till the muddy iron left the bottom with a rush, and she was free.

'Let go the sheet! Come for'ard again, and lend a hand on the chain! Stand by to give her the jib!' 'Frisco Kid, the boy who mooned over a picture of a girl in a magazine, had vanished, and 'Frisco Kid the sailor, strong and dominant, was on deck. He ran aft and tacked about as the jib rattled aloft in the hands of Joe, who quickly joined him. Just then the *Reindeer*, like a monstrous bat, passed to leeward of them in the gloom.

'Ah! dose boys! Dey take all-a night!' they heard Pete exclaim; and then the gruff voice of Nelson, who said: 'Never you mind, Frenchy. I learned the Kid his sailorising, and I ain't never been ashamed of him yet.'

The *Reindeer* was the faster boat, but by spilling the wind from her sails they managed so that the boys could keep them in sight. The breeze came steadily in from the west, with a promise of early increase. The stars were being blotted out by driving masses of clouds, which indicated a greater velocity in the upper strata. 'Frisco Kid surveyed the sky. 'Going to have it good and stiff before morning,' he prophesied, and Joe guessed so, too.

A couple of hours later both boats stood in for the land, and dropped anchor not more than a cable's length from the shore. A little wharf ran out, the bare end of which was perceptible to them, though they could discern a small yacht lying to a buoy a short distance away.

As on the previous night, everything was in readiness for hasty departure. The anchors could be tripped and the sails flung out on a moment's notice. Both skiffs came over noiselessly from the *Reindeer*. Nelson had given one of his two men to Pete, so that each skiff was doubly manned. They were not a very prepossessing bunch of men – at least, Joe thought so, for their faces bore a savage seriousness which almost made him shiver. The captain of the *Dazzler* buckled on his pistol belt and placed a rifle and a small double-block tackle in the boat. Nelson was also armed, while his men wore at their hips the customary sailor's sheath knife. They were very slow and careful to avoid noise in getting into the boats, Pete pausing long enough to warn the boys to remain quietly aboard and not try any tricks.

'Now'd be your chance, Joe, if they hadn't taken the skiffs,' 'Frisco Kid whispered, when the boats had vanished into the loom of the land.

'What's the matter with the *Dazzler*?' was the unexpected answer. 'We could up sail and away before you could say Jack Robinson.'

They crawled for'ard and began to hoist the mainsail. The anchor they could slip, if necessary, and save the time of pulling it up. But at the first rattle of the halyards on the sheaves a warning 'Hist!' came to them through the darkness, followed by a loudly whispered 'Drop that!'

Glancing in the direction from which these sounds proceeded, they made out a white face peering at them from over the rail of the other sloop.

'Aw, it's only the *Reindeer*'s boy,' 'Frisco Kid said. 'Come on.'

Again they were interrupted at the first rattling of the blocks.

'I say, you fellers, you'd better let go them halyards pretty quick, I'm a-tellin' you, or I'll give you what for!'

This threat being dramatically capped by the click of a cocking pistol, 'Frisco Kid obeyed and went grumbling back to the cockpit. 'Oh, there's plenty more chances to come,' he whispered consolingly to Joe. 'Pete was cute, wasn't he? Kind of thought you'd be trying to make a break, and fixed it so you couldn't.'

Nothing came from the shore to indicate how the pirates were faring. Not a dog barked, not a light flared; yet the air seemed quivering with an alarm about to burst forth. The night had taken on a strained feeling of intensity, as though it held in store all kinds of terrible things. The boys felt this keenly as they huddled against each other in the cockpit and waited.

'You were going to tell me about your running away,' Joe ventured finally, 'and why you came back again.'

'Frisco Kid took up the tale at once, speaking in a muffled undertone close to the other's ear.

'You see, when I made up my mind to quit the life, there wasn't a soul to lend me a hand; but I knew that the only thing for me to do was to get ashore and find some kind of work, so I could study. Then I figured there'd be more chance in the country than in the city; so I gave Nelson the slip. I was on the *Reindeer* then – one night on the Alameda oyster beds, and headed back from the Bay. But they were all Portuguese farmers thereabouts, and none of them had work for me. Besides, it was in the wrong time of the year – winter. That shows how much I knew about the land.

'I'd saved up a couple of dollars, and I kept travelling back, deeper and deeper into the country, looking for work and buying bread and cheese, and such things, from the storekeepers. I tell you it was cold, nights, sleeping out without blankets, and I was always glad when morning came. But worse than that was the way everybody looked on me. They were all suspicious, and not a bit afraid to show it, and sometimes they'd sick their dogs on me and tell me to get along. Seemed as though there wasn't no place for me on the land. Then my money gave out, and just about the time I was good and hungry I got captured.'

'Captured! What for?'

'Nothing. Living, I suppose. I crawled into a haystack to sleep one night, because it was warmer, and along comes a village constable and arrests me for being a tramp. At first they thought I was a runaway, and telegraphed my description all over. I told them I didn't have no people, but they wouldn't believe me for a long while. And then, when nobody claimed me, the judge sent me to a boys' "refuge" in San Francisco.'

He stopped and peered intently in the direction of the shore. The darkness and the silence in which the men had been swallowed up were profound. Nothing was stirring save the rising wind.

'I thought I'd die in that "refuge." Just like being in jail. You were locked up and guarded like any prisoner. Even then, if I could have liked the other boys it wouldn't have been so bad. But they were mostly street boys of the worst sort, without one spark of manhood or one idea of square dealing and fair play. There was only one thing I did like, and that was the books. Oh, I did lots of reading, I tell you. But that couldn't make up for the rest. I wanted the freedom, and the sunlight, and the salt water. And what had I done to be kept in prison and herded with such a gang? Instead of doing wrong, I had tried to do good, to make myself better, and that's what I got for it. I wasn't old enough, you see.

'Sometimes I'd see the sunshine dancing on the water and showing white on the sails, and the *Reindeer* cutting through it just as you please, and I'd get that sick I wouldn't know hardly what I did. And then the boys would come against me with some of their meannesses, and I'd start in to lick the whole kit of them. Then the men in charge'd lock me up and punish me. After I couldn't stand it no longer, I watched my chance, and cut and run for it. Seemed as though there wasn't no place on the land for me, so I picked up with Pete and went back on the Bay. That's about all there is to it, though I'm going to try it again when I get a little older – old enough to get a square deal for myself.'

'You're going to go back on the land with me,' Joe said authoritatively, laying a hand on his shoulder; 'that's what you're going to do. As for——'

Bang! A revolver shot rang out from the shore. Bang! Bang! More guns were speaking sharply and hurriedly. A man's voice rose wildly on the air and died away. Somebody began to cry for help. Both boys were to their feet on the instant, hoisting the mainsail and getting everything ready to run. The *Reindeer* boy was doing likewise. A man, roused from his sleep on the yacht, thrust an excited head through the skylight, but withdrew it hastily at sight of the two stranger sloops. The intensity of waiting was broken, the time for action come.

12 Perilous Hours

Heaving in on the anchor chain till it was up and down, 'Frisco Kid and Joe ceased from their exertions. Everything was in readiness to give the *Dazzler* the jib and go. They strained their eyes in the direction of the shore. The clamour had died away, but here and there lights were beginning to flash. The creaking of a block and tackle came to their ears, and they heard Nelson's voice singing out 'Lower away!' and 'Cast off!'

'Pete forgot to oil it,' 'Frisco Kid commented, referring to the tackle.

'Takin' their time about it, ain't they?' the boy on the *Reindeer* called over to them, sitting down on the cabin and mopping his face after the exertion of hoisting the mainsail singlehanded.

'Guess they're all right,' 'Frisco Kid rejoined.

'Say, you,' the man on the yacht cried through the skylight, not venturing to show his head. 'You'd better go away.'

'And you'd better stay below and keep quiet,' was the response.

'We'll take care of ourselves. See you do the same,' replied the boy on the *Reindeer*.

'If I was only out of this, I'd show you,' the man threatened.

'Lucky for you you're not,' was the response.

'Here they come!'

The two skiffs shot out of the darkness and came alongside. Some kind of an altercation was going on, as Pete's shrill voice attested.

'No, no!' he cried. 'Put it on ze *Dazzler*. Ze *Reindeer* she sail too fast-a, and run away, oh, so queeck, and never more I see it. Put it on ze

Dazzler. Eh? W'at you say?'

'All right,' Nelson agreed. 'We'll whack up afterwards. But hurry up. Out with you, lads, and heave her up. My arm's broke.'

The men tumbled out, ropes were cast inboard, and all hands, with the exception of Joe, tailed on. The shouting of men, the sound of oars, and the rattling and slapping of blocks and sails, told that the men on shore were getting under way for the pursuit.

'Now!' Nelson commanded. 'All together! Don't let her come back or you'll smash the skiff. There she takes it! A long pull and a strong pull! Once again! And yet again! Get a turn there, somebody, and take a spell.'

Though the task was but half accomplished, they were exhausted by the strenuous effort, and hailed the rest eagerly. Joe glanced over the side to discover what the heavy object might be, and saw the vague outlines of a very small office safe.

'Now, all together! Take her on the run, and don't let her stop! Yo, ho! Heave, ho! Once again! And another! Over with her!'

Straining and gasping, with tense muscles and heaving chests, they brought the cumbersome weight over the side, rolled it on top of the rail, and lowered it into the cockpit on the run. The cabin doors were thrown apart, and it was moved along, end for end, till it lay on the cabin floor, snug against the end of the centreboard case. Nelson had followed it aboard to superintend. His left arm hung helpless at his side, and from the fingertips blood dripped with monotonous regularity. He did not seem to mind it, however; nor even the mutterings of the human storm he had raised ashore, and which, to judge by the sounds, was even now threatening to break upon them.

'Lay your course for the Golden Gate,' he said to Pete, as he turned to go. 'I'll try to stand by you; but if you get lost in the dark, I'll meet you outside, off the Farralones, in the morning.' He sprang into the skiff after the men, and, with a wave of his uninjured arm, cried heartily: 'And then it's Mexico, my jolly rovers – Mexico and summer weather!'

Just as the *Dazzler*, freed from her anchor, paid off under the jib and filled away, a dark sail loomed under her stern, barely missing the skiff in tow. The cockpit of the stranger was crowded with men, who raised their voices angrily at sight of the pirates. Joe had half a mind to run for'ard and cut the halyards so that they might be captured. As he had told Pete the day before, he had done nothing to be ashamed of, and was not afraid to go before a court of justice. But the thought of 'Frisco Kid restrained him. He wished to take him ashore with him, but in so doing he did not wish to take him to jail. So he began to experience a keen interest in the escape of the *Dazzler*, after all.

The pursuing sloop rounded up hurriedly to come about after them, and in the darkness fouled the yacht which lay at anchor. The man aboard of her, thinking that at last his time had come, let out one wild yell, and ran on deck, screaming for help. In the confusion of the collision Pete and the boys slipped away into the night.

The *Reindeer* had already disappeared, and by the time Joe and 'Frisco Kid had the running gear coiled down and everything in shape, they were standing out in open water. The wind was freshening constantly, and the *Dazzler* heeling a lively clip through the comparatively smooth water. Before an hour had passed, the lights of Hunter's Point were well on her starboard beam. 'Frisco Kid went below to make coffee, but Joe remained on deck, watching the lights of south San Francisco grow, and speculating on his destination. Mexico! They were going to sea in such a frail craft! Impossible! At least, it seemed so to him, for his conceptions of ocean travel were limited to steamers and full-rigged ships, and he did not know how the tiny fishing boats ventured the open sea. He was beginning to feel half sorry that he had not cut the halyards, and longed to ask Pete a thousand questions; but just as the first was on his lips, that worthy ordered him to go below and get some coffee, and then to turn in. He was followed shortly afterward by 'Frisco Kid, Pete remaining at his lonely task of beating down the Bay and out to sea. Twice Pete heard the waves buffeted back from some flying forefoot, and once he saw a sail to leeward on the opposite tack, which luffed sharply and came about at sight of him. But the darkness favoured, and he heard no more of it – perhaps because he worked into the wind closer by a point, and held on his way with a rebellious shaking after leech.

Shortly after dawn the boys were called and came sleepily on deck. The day had broken cold and grey, while the wind had attained half a gale. Joe noted with astonishment the white tents of the quarantine station on Angel Island. San Francisco lay a smoky blur on the southern horizon, while the night, still lingering on the western edge of the world, slowly withdrew before their eyes. Pete was just finishing a long reach into the Raccoon Strait, and, at the same time, studiously regarding a plunging sloop yacht half a mile astern.

'Dey t'ink to catch ze *Dazzler*, eh? Bah!' And he brought the craft in question about, laying a course straight for the Golden Gate.

The pursuing yacht followed suit. Joe watched her a few moments. She held an apparently parallel course to them, and forged ahead much faster.

'Why, at this rate they'll have us in no time!' he cried.

Pete laughed. 'You t'ink so? Bah! Dey outfoot; we outpoint. Dey are scared of ze wind; we wipe ze eye of ze wind. Ah! you wait – you see.'

'They're travelling ahead faster,' 'Frisco Kid explained, 'but we're sailing closer to the wind. In the end we'll beat them, even if they have the nerve to cross the bar, which I don't think they have. Look! See!'

Ahead could be seen the great ocean surges, flinging themselves skyward and bursting into roaring caps of smother. In the midst of it, now rolling her dripping bottom clear, now sousing her deck load of lumber far above the guards, a coasting steam schooner was lumbering heavily into port. It was magnificent, this battle between man and the elements. Whatever timidity he had entertained fled away, and Joe's nostrils began to dilate and his eyes to flash at the nearness of the impending struggle.

Pete called for his oilskins and sou'wester, and Joe also was equipped with a spare suit. Then he and 'Frisco Kid were sent below to lash and cleat the safe in place. In the midst of this task Joe glanced at the firm name gilt-lettered on the face of it, and read, *Bronson & Tate*. Why, that was his father and his father's partner. That was their safe, their money! 'Frisco Kid, nailing the last retaining cleat on the floor of the cabin, looked up and followed his fascinated gaze.

'That's rough, isn't it?' he whispered. 'Your father?'

Joe nodded. He could see it all now. They had run in to San Andreas, where his father worked the big quarries, and most probably the safe contained the wages of the thousand men or so whom his firm employed. 'Don't say anything,' he cautioned.

'Frisco Kid agreed knowingly. 'Pete can't read, anyway,' he added, 'and the chances are that Nelson won't know what your name is. But, just the same, it's pretty rough. They'll break it open and divide up as soon as they can, so I don't see what you're going to do about it.'

'Wait and see.' Joe had made up his mind that he would do his best to stand by his father's property. At the worst, it could only be lost; and that would surely be the case were he not along; while, being along, he at least held a fighting chance to save or to be in position to recover it. Responsibilities were showering upon him thick and fast. Three days before he had had but himself to consider. Then, in some subtle way, he had felt a certain accountability for 'Frisco Kid's future welfare; and after that, and still more subtly, he had become aware of duties which he owed to his position, to his sister, to his chums, and to friends. And now, by a most unexpected chain of circumstances, came the pressing need of service for his father's sake. It was a call upon his deepest strength, and he responded bravely. While the future might be doubtful, he had no doubt of himself; and this very state of mind, this self-confidence, by a generous alchemy, gave him added strength. Nor did he fail to be vaguely aware of it, and to grasp dimly at the truth that confidence breeds confidence – strength, strength.

'Now she takes it!' Pete cried.

Both lads ran into the cockpit. They were on the edge of the breaking bar. A huge forty-footer reared a foam-crested head far above them, stealing their wind for the moment and threatening to crush the tiny craft like an eggshell. Joe held his breath. It was the supreme moment. Pete luffed straight into it, and the *Dazzler* mounted the steep slope with a rush, poised a moment on the giddy summit, and fell into the yawning valley beyond. Keeping off in the intervals to fill the mainsail, and luffing into the combers, they worked their way across the dangerous stretch. Once they caught the tail end of a whitecap and were well-nigh smothered in the froth; but otherwise the sloop bobbed and ducked with the happy facility of a cork.

To Joe it seemed as though he had been lifted out of himself, out of the world. Ah, this was life! This was action! Surely it could not be the old, commonplace world he had lived in so long! The sailors, grouped on the steaming deck load of the steamer, waved their sou'-westers, nor, on the bridge, was the captain above expressing his admiration for the plucky craft.

'Ah! You see! You see!' Pete pointed astern.

The sloop yacht had been afraid to venture it, and was skirting back and forth on the inner edge of the bar. The chase was off. A pilot boat, running for shelter from the coming storm, flew by them like a frightened bird, passing the steamer as though the latter were standing still.

Half an hour later the *Dazzler* passed beyond the last smoking sea and was sliding up and down on the long Pacific swell. The wind had increased its velocity and necessitated a reefing down of jib and mainsail. Then she laid off again, full and free on the starboard tack, for the Farralones, thirty miles away. By the time breakfast was cooked and eaten they picked up the *Reindeer*, hove to and working offshore to the south and west. The wheel was lashed down, and there was not a soul on deck.

Pete complained bitterly against such recklessness. 'Dat is ze one fault of Nelson. He no care. He is afraid of not'ing. Some day he will die, oh, so vaire queeck! I know, I know.'

Three times they circled about the *Reindeer*, running under her weather quarter and shouting in chorus, before they brought anybody on deck. Sail was then made at once, and together the two cockleshells plunged away into the vastness of the Pacific. This was necessary, as 'Frisco Kid informed Joe in order to have an offing before the whole fury of the storm broke upon them. Otherwise they would be driven on the lee shore of the California coast. 'Grub and water,' he said, could be obtained by running in to the land when fine weather came. He also congratulated Joe upon the fact that he was not seasick – which circumstance likewise brought praise from Pete, and put him in better humour with his mutinous sailor.

'I'll tell you what we'll do,' 'Frisco Kid whispered, while cooking dinner. 'Tonight we'll drag Pete down——'

'Drag Pete down?'

'Yes, and tie him up good and snug – as soon as it gets dark. Then put out the lights and make a run for it. Get to port anyway, anywhere, just so long as we shake loose from Nelson. You'll save your father's money, and I'll go away somewhere, over on the other side of the world, and begin all over again.'

'Then we'll have to call it off, that's all.'

'Call what off?'

'Tying Pete up and running for it.'

'No, sir; that's decided upon.'

'Now, listen here: I'll not have a thing to do with it – I'll go on to Mexico first -- if you don't make me one promise.'

'And what's the promise?'

'Just this: you place yourself in my hands from the moment we get ashore, and trust to me. You don't know anything about the land, anyway – you said so. And I'll fix it with my father – I know I can – so that you can get to study, and get an education, and be something else than a Bay pirate or a sailor. That's what you'd like, isn't it?'

Though he said nothing, 'Frisco Kid showed how well he liked it by the expression of his face.

'And it'll be no more than your due, either,' Joe continued. 'You've stood by me, and you'll have recovered my father's money. He'll owe it to you.'

'But I don't do things that way. Think I do a man a favour just to be paid for it?'

'Now you keep quiet. How much do you think it'd cost my father to recover that safe? Give me your promise, that's all, and when I've got things arranged, if you don't like them you can back out. Come on; that's fair.'

They shook hands on the bargain and proceeded to map out their line of action for the night.

But the storm yelling down out of the northwest had something entirely different in store for the *Dazzler* and her crew. By the time dinner was over they were forced to put double reefs in mainsail and jib, and still the gale had not reached its height. The sea, also, had been kicked up till it was a continuous succession of water mountains, frightful and withal grand to look upon from the low deck of the sloop. It was only when the sloops were tossed up on the crests of the waves at the same time that they caught sight of each other. Occasional fragments of seas swashed into the cockpit or dashed aft clear over the cabin, and before long Joe was stationed at the small pump to keep the well dry.

At three o'clock, watching his chance, Pete motioned to the *Reindeer* that he was going to heave to and get out a sea anchor. This latter was of the nature of a large shallow canvas bag, with the mouth held open by triangularly lashed spars. To this the towing ropes were attached, on the kite principle, so that the greatest resisting surface was presented to the water. The sloop, drifting so much faster, would thus be held bow on to both wind and sea – the safest possible position in a storm. Nelson waved his hand in response that he understood, and to go ahead.

Pete went for'ard to launch the sea anchor himself, leaving it to 'Frisco Kid to put the helm down at the proper moment and run into the wind.

The Frenchman poised on the slippery foredeck, waiting an opportunity. But at this the moment the *Dazzler* lifted into an unusually large sea, and, as she cleared the summit, caught a heavy snort of the gale at the very instant she was righting herself to an even keel.

Thus there was not the slightest yield to this sudden pressure coming on her sails and mast gear.

Snap! Crash! The steel weather rigging was carried away at the lanyards, and mast, jib, mainsail, blocks, stays, sea anchor, Pete – everything -- went over the side. Almost by a miracle, the captain clutched at the bobstay and managed to get one hand up and over the bowsprit. The boys ran for'ard to drag him into safety, and Nelson, observing the disaster, put up his helm and instantly ran the *Reindeer* down to the rescue of the imperilled crew.

13   The End of the Cruise

Pete was uninjured from the fall overboard with the *Dazzler*'s mast, but the sea anchor which had gone with him had not escaped so easily. The gaff of the mainsail had been driven through it, and it refused to work. The wreckage, thumping alongside, held the sloop in a quartering slant to the seas – not so dangerous a position as it might be, nor as safe, either.

'Goodbye, old-a *Dazzler*. Never no more you wipe ze eye of ze wind. Never no more you kick your heels at ze crack gentleman yachts.'

So the captain lamented, standing in the cockpit and surveying the ruin with wet eyes. Even Joe, who bore him great dislike, felt sorry for him at this moment. As the horse is to the Arab, so the ship is to the sailor, and Pete suffered his loss keenly. A heavier blast of the wind caught the jagged crest of a wave and hurled it upon the helpless craft.

'Can't we save her?' Joe spluttered.

'Frisco Kid shook his head.

'Or the safe?'

'Impossible,' he answered. 'Couldn't lay another boat alongside for a United States mint. As it is, it'll keep us guessing to save ourselves.'

Another sea swept over them, and the skiff, which had long since been swamped, dashed itself to pieces against the stern. Then the *Reindeer* towered above them on a mountain of water. Joe caught himself half shrinking back, for it seemed she would fall down squarely on top of them; but the next instant she dropped into the gaping trough, and they were looking down upon her far below. It was a striking picture – one Joe was destined never to forget. The *Reindeer* was wallowing in the snow-white smother, her rails flush with the sea, the water scudding across her deck in foaming cataracts. The air was filled with flying spray, which made the scene appear hazy and unreal. One of the men was clinging to the perilous afterdeck and striving to cast off the waterlogged skiff. The boy, leaning far over the cockpit rail and holding on for dear life, was passing him a knife. The second man stood at the wheel, putting it up with flying hands, and forcing the sloop to pay off. By him, his injured arm in a sling, was Nelson, his sou'wester gone and his fair hair plastered in wet, wind-blown ringlets about his face. His whole attitude breathed indomitability, courage, strength. Joe looked upon him in sudden awe, and, realising the enormous possibilities in the man, felt sorrow for the way in which they had been wasted. A pirate – a robber! In that flashing moment he caught a glimpse of truth, grasped at the mystery of success and failure. Of such stuff as Nelson were heroes made; but they possessed wherein he lacked – the power of choice, the careful poise of mind, the sober control of soul.

These were the thoughts which came to Joe in the flight of a second. Then the *Reindeer* swept skyward and hurtled across their bow to leeward on the breast of a mighty billow.

'Ze wild man! Ze wild man!' Pete shrieked, watching her in amazement. 'He t'inks he can gybe! He will die! We will all die! He must come about! Oh, ze fool! Ze fool!'

But time was precious, and Nelson ventured the chance. At the right moment he gybed the mainsail over and hauled back on the wind.

'Here she comes! Make ready to jump for it!' 'Frisco Kid cried to Joe.

The *Reindeer* dashed by their stern, heeling over till the cabin windows were buried, and so close that it appeared she must run them down. But a freak of the waters lurched the two crafts apart. Nelson, seeing that the manœuvre has miscarried, instantly instituted another. Throwing the helm hard up, the *Reindeer* whirled on her heel, thus swinging her overhanging main boom closer to the *Dazzler*. Pete was the nearest, and the opportunity could last no longer than a second. Like a cat he sprang, catching the footrope with both hands. Then the *Reindeer* forged ahead, dipping him into the sea at every plunge. But he clung on, working inboard every time he emerged, till he dropped into the cockpit, as Nelson squared off to run down to leeward and repeat the manœuvre.

'Your turn next,' 'Frisco Kid said.

'No, yours,' Joe replied.

'But I know more about the water,' 'Frisco Kid insisted.

'I can swim as well as you,' said the other.

It would have been hard to forecast the outcome of this dispute; but, as it was, the swift rush of events made any settlement useless. The *Reindeer* had gybed over and was ploughing back at breakneck speed, careening at such an angle that it seemed she must surely capsize. It was a gallant sight.

The storm burst in fury, the shouting wind flattening the ragged crests till they boiled. The *Reindeer* dipped from view behind an immense wave. The wave rolled on, but where the sloop had been the boys noted with startled eyes only the angry waters. Doubting, they looked a second time. There was no *Reindeer*. They were alone on the ocean.

'God have mercy on their souls!'

Joe was too horrified at the suddenness of the catastrophe to utter a sound.

'Sailed her clean under, and, with the ballast she carried, went straight to bottom,' 'Frisco Kid gasped when he could speak. 'Pete always said Nelson would drown himself that way someday! And now they're all gone. It's dreadful – dreadful. But now we've got to look out for ourselves, I tell you! The back of the storm broke in that puff, but the sea'll kick up worse yet as the wind eases down. Lend a hand, and hang on with the other. We've got to get her head on.'

Together, knives in hand, they crawled for'ard, where the pounding wreckage hampered the boat sorely. 'Frisco Kid took the lead in the ticklish work, but Joe obeyed orders like a veteran. Every minute or so the bow was swept by the sea, and they were pounded and buffeted about like a pair of shuttlecocks. First the main portion of the wreckage was securely fastened to the for'ard bitts; then, breathless and gasping, more often under the water than out, it was cut and hack at the tangle of halyards, sheets, stays, and tackles. The cockpit was taking water rapidly, and it was a race between swamping and completing the task. At last, however, everything stood clear save the lee rigging. 'Frisco Kid slashed the lanyards. The storm did the rest. The *Dazzler* drifted swiftly to leeward of the wreckage, till the strain on the line fast to the for'ard bitts jerked her bow into place, and she ducked dead into the eye of the wind and sea.

Pausing but for a cheer at the success of their undertaking, the two lads raced aft, where the cockpit was half full and the dunnage of the cabin all afloat. With a couple of buckets procured from the stern lockers, they proceeded to fling the water overboard. It was heart-breaking work, for many a barrelful was flung back upon them again; but they persevered, and when night fell, the *Dazzler*, bobbing merrily at her sea anchor, could boast that her pumps sucked once more. As 'Frisco Kid had said, the backbone of the storm was broken, though the wind had veered to the west, where it still blew stiffly.

'If she holds,' 'Frisco Kid said, referring to the breeze, 'we'll drift to the California coast, somewhere long in, tomorrow. There's nothing to do now but wait.'

They said little, oppressed by the loss of their comrades and overcome with exhaustion, preferring to huddle against each other for the sake of warmth and companionship. It was a miserable night, and they shivered constantly from the cold. Nothing dry was to be obtained aboard, food, blankets, everything being soaked with the salt water. Sometimes they dozed; but these intervals were short and harassing, for it seemed as if each of the two boys took turns in waking with such a sudden start as to rouse the other.

At last day broke, and they looked about. Wind and sea had dropped considerably, and there was no question as to the safety of the *Dazzler*. The coast was nearer than they had expected, its cliffs showing dark and forbidding in the grey of dawn. But with the rising of the sun they could see the yellow beaches, flanked by the white surf, and, beyond – it seemed too good to be true – the clustering houses and smoking chimneys of a town.

'It's Santa Cruz!' 'Frisco Kid cried. 'And we'll run no risk of being wrecked in the surf!'

'Then you think we'll save the safe?' Joe queried.

'Yes, indeed we will! There isn't much of a sheltered harbour for large vessels, but with this breeze we'll run right up the mouth of the San Lorenzo River. Then there's a little lake like, and boathouses. Water smooth as glass. Come on. We'll be in in time for breakfast.'

Bringing to light some spare coils of rope from the lockers, he put a clove hitch on the standing part of the sea-anchor hawser, and carried the new running line aft, making it fast to the stern bitts. Then he cast off from the for'ard bitts. Naturally the *Dazzler* swung off into the trough, completed the evolution, and pointed her nose toward shore. A couple of spare oars from below, and as many water-soaked blankets, sufficed to make a jury mast and sail. When this was in place Joe cast loose from the wreckage, which was now towing astern, while 'Frisco Kid took the tiller.

'How's that?' said 'Frisco Kid, as he finished making the *Dazzler* fast fore and aft, and stepped upon the string-piece of the tiny wharf. 'What'll we do next, captain?'

Joe looked up in quick surprise. 'Why – I – what's the matter?'

'Well, aren't you captain now? Haven't we reached land? I'm crew from now on, you know. What's your orders?'

Joe caught the spirit of it. 'Pipe all hands for breakfast; that is – wait a minute.'

Diving below, he possessed himself of the money he had stowed away in his bundle when he came aboard. Then he locked the cabin door, and they went uptown in search of restaurants. Over the breakfast Joe planned the next move, and, when they had done, communicated it to 'Frisco Kid.

In response to his inquiry the cashier told him when the morning train started for San Francisco. He glanced at the clock.

'I've just time to catch it,' he said to 'Frisco Kid. 'Here is the key to the cabin door. Keep it locked, and don't let anybody come aboard. Here's money. Eat at the restaurants. Dry your blankets and sleep in the cockpit. I'll be back tomorrow. And don't let anybody into that cabin. Goodbye.'

With a hasty handgrip, he sped down the street to the depot. The conductor, when he punched his ticket, looked at him with surprise. And well he might, for it was not the custom of his passengers to travel in sea boots and sou'westers. But Joe did not mind. He did not even notice. He had bought a paper and was absorbed in its contents.

SUPPOSED TO HAVE BEEN LOST

The tug *Sea Queen*, chartered by Bronson & Tate, has returned from a fruitless cruise outside the heads. No news of value could be obtained concerning the pirates who so daringly carried off their safe at San Andreas last Tuesday night. The lighthouse keeper at the Farralones mentions having sighted the two sloops Wednesday morning, clawing offshore in the teeth of the gale. It is supposed by shipping men that they have perished in the storm with their ill-gotten treasure. Rumour has it that, in addition to a large sum in gold, the safe contained papers of even greater importance.

When Joe had read this he felt a great relief. It was evident no one had been killed at San Andreas on the night of the robbery, else there would have been some comment on it in the paper. Nor, if they had had any clue to his own whereabouts, would they have omitted such a striking bit of information.

At the depot in San Francisco the curious onlookers were surprised to see a boy clad conspicuously in sea boots and sou'wester hail a cab and dash away in it. But Joe was in a hurry. He knew his father's hours, and was fearful lest he should not catch him before he went to luncheon.

The office boy scowled at him when he pushed open the door and asked to see Mr Bronson; nor could the head clerk, when summoned by this strange-looking intruder, recognise him.

'Don't you know me, Mr Willis?'

Mr Willis looked a second time. 'Why, it's Joe Bronson! Of all things under the sun, where did you drop from? Go right in. Your father's in there.'

Mr Bronson stopped dictating to his stenographer, looked up, and said: 'Hello! where have you been?'

'To sea,' Joe answered demurely enough, not sure of just what kind of a reception he was to get, and fingering his sou'wester nervously.

'Short trip, eh? How did you make out?'

'Oh, so-so.' He had caught the twinkle in his father's eye, and knew that it was all clear sailing. 'Not so bad – er – that is, considering.'

'Considering?'

'Well, not exactly that; rather, it might have been worse, and, well – I don't know that it could have been better.'

'You interest me; sit down.' Then, turning to the stenographer, 'You may go, Mr Brown, and – hum – I shan't need you any more today.'

It was all Joe could do to keep from crying, so kindly and naturally had his father received him – making him feel at once as if not the slightest thing uncommon had occurred. It was as if he had just returned from a vacation, or, man grown, had come back from some business trip.

'Now go ahead, Joe. You were speaking to me a moment ago in conundrums, and have aroused my curiosity to a most uncomfortable degree.'

Thereat Joe sat down and told what had happened, all that had happened, from the previous Monday night to that moment. Each little incident he related, every detail, not forgetting his conversations with 'Frisco Kid nor his plans concerning him. His face flushed and he was carried away with the excitement of the narrative, while Mr Bronson was almost as interested, urging him on whenever he slackened his pace, but otherwise remaining silent.

'So you see,' Joe said at last, 'it couldn't possibly have turned out any better.'

'Ah, well,' Mr Bronson deliberated judiciously, 'it may be so, and then again it may not.'

'I don't see it.' Joe felt sharp disappointment at his father's qualified approval. It seemed to him that the return of the safe merited something stronger.

That Mr Bronson fully comprehended the way Joe felt about it was clearly in evidence, for he went on: 'As to the matter of the safe, all hail to you, Joe. Credit, and plenty of it, is your due. Mr Tate and I have already spent five hundred dollars in attempting to recover it. So important was it that we have also offered five thousand dollars reward, and this morning were even considering the advisability of increasing the amount. But, my son' – Mr Bronson stood up, resting a hand affectionately on his boy's shoulder – 'there be certain things in this world which are of still greater importance than gold or papers which represent that which gold may buy. How about *yourself*? There's the point. Will you sell the best possibilities of your life right now for a million dollars?'

Joe shook his head.

'As I said, that's the point. A human life the treasure of the world cannot buy; nor can it redeem one which is misspent; nor can it make full and complete and beautiful a life which is dwarfed and warped and ugly. How about yourself? What is to be the effect of all these strange adventures on your life – *your* life, Joe? Are you going to pick yourself up tomorrow and try it over again? Or the next day, or the day after? Do you understand? Why, Joe, do you think for one moment that I could place against the best value of my son's life the paltry value of a safe? And *can* I say, until time has told me, whether this trip of yours could not possibly have been better? Such an experience is as potent for evil as for good. One dollar is exactly like another – there are many in the world; but no Joe is like my Joe, nor can there be any others in the world to take his place. Don't you see, Joe? Don't you understand?'

Mr Bronson's voice broke slightly, and the next instant Joe was sobbing as though his heart would break. He had never understood this father of his before, and he knew now the pain he must have caused him, to say nothing of his mother and sister. But the four

It was the supreme moment

stirring days he had spent had given him a clearer view of the world and humanity, and he had always possessed the power of putting his thoughts into speech; so he spoke of these things and the lessons he had learned, the conclusions he had drawn from his conversations with 'Frisco Kid, from his talks with Pete, from the graphic picture he retained of the *Reindeer* and Nelson as they wallowed in the trough beneath him. And Mr Bronson listened and, in turn, understood.

'But what of 'Frisco Kid, father?' Joe asked when he had finished.

'Hum! There's a great deal of promise in the boy, from what you say of him.' Mr Bronson hid the twinkle in his eye this time. 'And, I must confess, he seems perfectly capable of shifting for himself.'

'Sir?' Joe could not believe his ears.

'Let us see, then. He is at present entitled to the half of five thousand dollars, the other half of which belongs to you. It was you two who preserved the safe from the bottom of the Pacific, and if you only had waited a little longer, Mr Tate and I might have increased the reward.'

'Oh!' Joe caught a glimmering of the light. 'Part of that is easily arranged, father. I simply refuse to take my half. As to the other – that isn't exactly what 'Frisco Kid desires. He wants friends – and – and – though you didn't say so, they are far higher than gold, nor can gold buy them. He wants friends and a chance for an education – not twenty-five hundred dollars.'

'Don't you think it would be better that he choose for himself?'

'Ah, no. That's all arranged.'

'Arranged?'

'Yes, sir. He's captain on sea, and I'm captain on land. So he's under my charge now.'

'Then you have the power of attorney for him in the present negotiations? Good. I'll make a proposition. The twenty-five hundred dollars shall be held in trust by me, on his demand at any time. We'll settle about yours afterward. Then he shall be put on probation for, say, a year – as messenger first, and then in the office. You can either coach him in his studies, or he can attend night school. And after that, if he comes through his period of probation with flying colours, I'll give him the same opportunities for an education that you possess. It all depends on himself. And now, Mr Attorney, what have you to say to my offer in the interests of your client?'

'That I close with it at once – and thank you.' Father and son shook hands.

'And what are you going to do now, Joe?'

'I'm going to send a telegram to 'Frisco Kid first, and then hurry home.'

'Then wait a minute till I call up San Andreas and tell Mr Tate the good news, and I'll go with you.'

'Mr Willis,' Mr Bronson said as they left the outer office, 'do you remain in charge, and kindly tell the clerks that they are free for the rest of the day.

'And I say,' he called back as they entered the elevator, 'don't forget the office boy.'